CHOSEN BY BLOOD

COURT OF MAGIC: VAMPIRES OF MIST

LACEY CARTER ANDERSEN
MELANIE GREY

DEDICATION

To my husband-- who plays Overcooked with me, makes me smile, and always remembers to say he loves me.

~ Lacey Carter Andersen

To the coffee that kept me going this last month.

~ Melanie Grey

WANT MORE FROM LACEY CARTER ANDERSEN?

Want to be part of the writing process? Maybe even get a taste of my sense of humor? Teasers for my new releases? And more? Join Lacey's Realm on Facebook!

1

28 years ago...

FELICITY

THIS PLACE WAS CURSED. Mist always had been, and the knowledge left me unsettled as I drove through the stormy night to a destination that might be even more dangerous than where I am now.

Mist was a town where many supernaturals had been murdered over the years, mostly by supernatural hunters. Humans hell-bent on wiping out the other races. It was said that all the great hunters had been born in Mist, and had slaughtered the other races day after day, leaving behind so many miserable souls that the entire town was filled with the ghosts of the dead.

But all things changed with time. And as everyone knows, the supernaturals wouldn't stay hidden in the shadows much longer, and the humans would regret pissing them off.

After the slaughter of the supernaturals, the magic races rose up against humanity. Humans were hunted like livestock. And many of our people brought their victims here as a way of honoring their family members who had been murdered so cruelly.

So ghosts, human and supernatural alike, gathered in this cursed place. They filled the air with what humans saw as a Mist, hence the name of this place, but that we could see as spirits, chained to forever roam these miserable lands.

My hands tightened on my steering wheel as thunder roared overhead and rain unleashed above my car, making it even harder to see the road through the dark and the mist.

At any other time, I wouldn't have left my warm bed. I would've avoided these dangerous roads and this dangerous night. Only one thing could compel me to take this risk, and it was a command from Lady Darkmore herself.

Even though I lived alone, separate from the powerful vampire coven, I had heard the news of the birth of her twins. What I didn't understand was why she needed a Seer tonight. The twins should have been enough of a miracle. Vampires, as far as we knew, couldn't have children. Lady Darkmore must have made a deal with the devil himself to birth her own children, rather than finding human children to adopt and Turning them at the right age, as the government allowed, with permission.

Perhaps that's why I was being called. Her deal had consequences that she only now thought to fear. Still, I would've preferred not to be involved with any of this.

It was trouble. Even without my powers, I knew it.

"But no one refuses a Darkmore," I whispered to myself.

Above me, the thunder boomed as if in agreement. I

found the right road and drove slowly up until I came to the huge gates that looked oddly similar to what I imagined the gates of hell to look like, other than the giant "D" that split apart as the gate opened in front of me.

When I could, I inched forward, continuing down the long driveway surrounded by trees. Up ahead, the foliage seemed to part, revealing the massive manor. I swore every light was turned on inside.

Out on the steps, two vampires waited for me.

I stopped my car near the bottom of the steps and took a deep breath. Whatever the powerful lady wanted from me, I would give it to her. The Darkmores weren't just feared because they ruled all the houses in Mist. It was also because their bloodline had both vampire and fae running through it. Not fairies. Fairies were sweet, liked glitter, and cupcakes. Fae...fae liked power. Fae never shied away from death. And the fae could do things that few other races could compete with.

This was a time to be very careful.

Taking a deep breath, I opened my door, but no rain fell on me. I looked up to find a vampire, with red rings around blue eyes, holding an umbrella for me. "Ms. Sona, our lady waits."

I was shaking as I closed my car door and followed him up the steps. Two vampires were suddenly on both sides of the doors to the manor and parted them at my approach.

"This way," the vampire with the umbrella said, handing it to one of the two doormen as we swept into the massive foyer, with its two sprawling staircases on each side.

We took one of the staircases up to the second story, and then continued all the way to the back of the house where a quiet vampire opened a door for me. Inside, was clearly the Darkmore's bedroom. It was a strange mix between archaic and modern, with white marble, a massive bed, with a huge headboard, and a fire dancing in a fireplace to one side of the room. In the bed, was Lady Darkmore herself, her pale, almost white, hair loose around her shoulders in a way I'd never seen before. She wore a white nightgown, and her huge husband stood at her side.

His dark eyes found me immediately, and his shoulders went back. "Seer, we are grateful you were able to come so quickly."

That was one thing I always liked about the Darkmores. While they knew no one could refuse them, they were hardly the tyrants their parents were before them. Yes, they still killed the occasional human. Yes, they preferred warm blood, straight from the source, but they also kept a firm hold on their people, working hard to keep their presence hidden from the humans who believed no supernaturals lived amongst them in this town.

"Of course," I said, finally finding my voice and bowing. "What do you need of me?"

Lady Darkmore rose from her bed, and her husband instantly wrapped his arms around her, lending her support. I had never seen the great lady as anything but a creature nearly made of stone. She never smiled. She never showed weakness. But here, she looked like any other woman after having given birth. Tired. Exhausted even. As they headed toward two bassinets.

When they stopped beside the white cradles, lightning flashed behind them, and I jumped a little. The two huge doors that connected to their balcony were closed tightly, but the raging storm seemed determined to break in.

Lady Darkmore finally looked at me, those strange hazel eyes of hers worried. "Can you check my babies? Can you tell me anything about Liam and Dawn's futures?"

"Of course," I said, but that sixth sense of mine whispered that this was more than just a nervous mother. "Is there something specific that you would like me to...check for?"

She didn't answer me, so I inched closer to the children. For some strange reason, I felt like I was in a den of wolves, and that one wrong move toward the babies would get me killed. Maybe it was that the children's existence should be impossible, or the stormy night, but my instincts were screaming to be careful.

When I finally caught sight of them, my breath hitched. The boy was sleeping peacefully. He had a head of dark hair, and his features were soft in sleep. He was a beautiful baby. Large and strong-looking, just like his father. Until this moment, I hadn't actually believed that a vampire could have a child, but maybe the fae within Lady Darkmore was enough to create this miracle.

And then, I looked at the other child and froze.

There was something wrong with her. I knew this immediately. She had a head full of hair the same white-blonde as her mother's, maybe even a lighter shade, if that was possible. And hazel eyes rimmed by red stared up at me, far too acutely. Like she was evaluating me just as I was evaluating her. While with the boy child I sensed calmness and a child-like innocent, with this girl...it felt like I was staring at something wrong. Something, not quite evil, but something that disturbed me.

"She isn't normal," the mother finally said, and she sounded like a terrified mother rather than a powerful vampire. "The midwife suggested we kill her..."

A rushed breath escaped my lips. "Don't kill a baby."

"We never would," the father said, his voice low and

menacing. "And the midwife was promptly thrown from the balcony for even suggesting such a thing."

Fuck. Okay, I definitely have to be careful here.

"So, can you use your gifts?" Lady Darkmore asked. "Can you tell us what her powers are? What her future holds?"

Sweat ran down my back. "I'll try."

They nodded and the father steered her a step away from the babies.

I was rattled, but I tried not to show it. If I gave into my fear of this powerful couple, my powers might not work, and then I wasn't sure what they would do. So, I took several deep breaths and reached out to gently set a hand on each baby. Maybe they only cared about the girl child, but twins were rare in the supernatural world. Whatever was happening with the girl baby would somehow be connected to the boy.

The second I closed my eyes, images assaulted me. I gasped and struggled to stay standing. It felt like being in the center of a tornado while the future swirled around me. I saw them, the children as they grew. The boy was pure goodness. With his hands, he would heal. Everything he touched would be filled with that goodness inside of him.

He would change Mist. It was possible that he would change the world.

Although I sensed his life would be short.

It was like watching something too beautiful to exist. I was distantly aware that I was crying, but I couldn't take my eyes off the young man. And then, his face faded away and darkness swallowed me. The tornado of images stopped, and then I saw a young girl with pure white hair. In her eyes was loneliness. Pain. Suffering so deep that no child should know what it felt like to be that way.

I knelt down. "What is it, sweety?"

Her hands reached out and death spread from them. Flowers bent and withered away. Animals died. And then the sound of people suffering came from all around me.

"I'll only bring death," she whispered. "Death is all I will ever be."

I rushed away from her, torn between wanting to comfort her and fearing her. "No," I whispered. "You're more than death. I know it."

And then, I saw it. There was something inside of her. A light nearly swallowed by the darkness. *What was the light?*

"Everything I touch dies," she whispered, and the tornado swept her away, and images flashed around me, so fast I felt sick.

When my eyes opened, I found myself still standing above the two babies. The girl still watched me as I cautiously drew my hands back.

"What did you see?" Lord Darkmore said.

I wiped the tears from my face and chose my words with care. "Your son will be a healer. Healers are rare and sacred. He will be a light in a dark world."

"And the girl?" They both seemed to be holding their breath.

I wouldn't tell them it all. No, if I did, they might just end her life now. But I would tell them the most important thing. "One day, her touch will bring death. Not all the time, but when her emotions overwhelm her. She could...she could be a powerful tool for the Darkmore House, but she must be treated with care."

Lady Darkmore pressed her hand to her mouth, and tears filled her eyes.

Lord Darkmore moved to his daughter's bassinet and looked down. I held my breath, wondering what he would do with such a dangerous creature. "Dawn is our daughter. She might be death itself, but she is a Darkmore. She is *ours*."

I nodded. "And I saw goodness in her." They both looked at me. "A light beyond the darkness."

"Thank you," Lord Darkmore said.

And they turned their backs on me, staring down at the children.

The room was tense as I left. A vampire led me to my car, and I switched my engine on with shaking hands. As I drove away from the manor, I told myself it was time to leave Mist.

Whatever happened with this girl, I wasn't sure she was strong enough to find that spark of goodness inside her. And if she didn't, I truly believed that she'd be the death of us all.

And yet? What did that spark mean? I hated that some secret sense inside of me said that as long as her brother lived, she would need to be the darkness that balanced him. *Because...because what would happen when he died? Would the spark finally be allowed to shine?*

I shivered. *I don't know, but I won't be here to find out.*

2

EIGHTEEN YEARS LATER...

Aiden

STRUGGLING, I fought within the sack that had been thrown around me, but the fact that my wrists and ankles were still tied behind me made it impossible. I shouted around the gag in my mouth, then felt myself thrown down onto a hard surface.

My mind raced. Who the hell would've taken me? My foster father had disappeared. I was just a kid in high school, who would want me dead?

The answer came easily: probably a supernatural that wanted to feed off of a human.

My blood ran cold.

A minute later, the sack was pulled off of me, and I was blinking into a bright light. Something sharp struck the side of my neck, and an indescribably awful pain, like being electrocuted, shot through my neck. My vision went black, and I could feel tears rolling down my face.

I don't know when I came back to myself, but my hands and feet were no longer bound the same way. Instead, I'd been strapped to what looked like an operating table. My heart raced, and a man's face suddenly hovered above mine.

"I'm human," I rasped. "I'm a protected race. You can't hurt me."

It was true, except it might not help me. Because as hard as the government tried to protect humans, our numbers were declining so rapidly for a reason. With so many of the supernaturals seeing us as a food source, even the harsh punishments for hurting us wasn't enough to stop the worst of the other races. Yet, some small part of me still hoped it would stop the smiling man above me.

He didn't look the least bit concerned as he grabbed a fistful of my hair and jerked my head back. "In your realm, humans are weak. They have no skills to protect themselves. And one day, no doubt, all of you will be dead."

"Realm?" *Was this guy insane? What the hell was a realm?*

He laughed. "I forgot how little your people know. This primitive realm is pathetic. In every single way. Which, of course, made this the perfect place for us to go. But yes, you ignorant fool, there are different realms. Different worlds that are like yours, only not exactly. And with enough magic, warlocks can step between these realms."

"Warlocks?" I hated how stupid I sounded. "Warlocks aren't real. Humans can't have powers."

He jerked my head back a little again and slapped my cheek, almost playfully, but it hurt all the same. "Warlocks are real, boy. Not in your realm, but in most of the others. Humans had new genes unlocked that allowed them to use magic. No one is sure how this happened, but they've been trying to replicate it for many years. But having these powers is one of the only reasons we're not facing extinction like the humans of your realm."

I felt sick. "Okay, I believe you. But why take me? If we're both...human, in a sense, then why do all of this?"

"Humans and warlocks are not the same," he said, a bitter note to his voice. "We are an evolved form of you. It's like calling a human a monkey. It's insulting."

"Sorry," I blurted out. No, I didn't believe all this warlock nonsense, but I also didn't want this unstable guy to hurt me.

"Don't be sorry. Accept that you will be a part of a wonderful experiment to give humans even more of a fighting chance at survival." He truly sounded like one of those cackling villains in kid's shows. "My master has commanded me to help humanity achieve the next step in its evolution. And you, Aiden, will be part of this epic process."

"Me? What do I have to do with any of this?"

He leaned in closer, so close that his breath puffed across my face. "When we're done with you, there will be nothing human about you."

My breathing was ragged. "No. I don't want to do this. I'd rather just stay a human. Please, let me go."

His hand holding my hair slammed my head back so hard on the table that my vision wavered, and I could feel blood begin pouring out of the back of my skull. Reaching down, he did something, while my head rang. Then, pulled back his fingers to show that they were now covered in my blood. He smeared the blood across my forehead and began to murmur words that were obviously some kind of spell, or perhaps just an insane man's ritual.

But the blood on my forehead...it began to burn. Hotter and hotter.

He stopped his spell and smiled once more. "If you survive this, you'll be the first hybrid of your kind." When he released my hair, my head rolled to the side, and a scream caught in the back of my throat. On the side of the room, body after body had been stacked up. And every body looked horrifying. Like a terrible spell gone wrong.

He began to murmur again, and this time, my entire body began to burn.

The last thing I was aware of was my own screaming and his laughter.

3

Dawn

My phone rang, and I jerked my gaze away from the headstone. With shaking hands, I reached into my pocket and saw Sammi's name on the screen. My old friend was just about the only person I wanted to talk to right now.

"Hello?" I said, my greeting sounded pained, even to my own ears.

"Hi," her voice was soft and gentle.

Rain pattered on my clear umbrella overhead, seeming louder in the silence between our words, and I forced myself to breathe calmly. Even while the mournful howling of the ghosts began again, sending a chill down my spine, I tried to keep control of my emotions. Which was damned hard. The sound reflected the way I felt...like my soul had been torn from my chest, but I was still left to wander the earth in misery.

"I'm so sorry I couldn't make it to the funeral. Work got in the way."

"It's okay." I tried to sound cheery and failed. I would never have expected Sammi to be able to be here. She'd worked so hard to become a Human Defender that I couldn't see her taking off time from work, no matter the reason.

"How are you?"

"How am I?" The words seemed to echo in my mind. "My brother is dead. My best friend is dead." My words cracked.

"Geez, I'm such an idiot. Of course, I shouldn't have asked how you were. But I did want you to know that I'll be looking into his murder."

I shook my head. "Don't bother. We're going to figure it out. The bastard that tore him to pieces didn't leave a lot of clues, but my brother's death will be avenged, I promise you that."

Sammi was human. And she thought I was human too. So, I couldn't exactly tell her that my family wasn't just the wealthiest family in Mist, as she'd always believed, but that we were vampires. And another supernatural had been responsible for my brother's death, which meant that someone would be paying with his or her life.

"Of course," she said. "Just...as a Human Defender I have skills--"

"No. Thank you though."

The last thing we needed was to have a Human Defender stomping around our lands. With all of Sammi's experience now, she would be able to figure out pretty quickly that this town, which was supposed to be forbidden to supernaturals, was full of us. As much as I wished I could take her up on her offer, she'd only get us into more trouble. Her priority was protecting humans from the other races, not protecting supernaturals from each other.

"Okay, well, let me know if I can do anything else. Seriously. Even though I can't be *there* there, I'm always here."

"Thanks." I sounded as numb as I felt.

"Okay, I better go. Apparently, an orc is throwing a tantrum in a subway. I have to take care of it before anyone gets hurt."

"Of course. Goodbye."

"Goodbye," she said, and she sounded as sad as I felt.

Turning off my phone, I shoved it back into my pocket. The hairs on my arms suddenly stood on end, and I felt my lip curl. Damn it. I was being watched. I could feel it deep in my bones. My keen vampiric senses screamed, urging me to turn around and face whatever danger lurked in the shadows. Vampires had few predators, but the ones we had were not to be ignored.

But still, I remained rooted in place. *Because not even a threat against me matters today. Not here.* Any comfort I felt from Sammi's call faded away, replaced by my bone-deep misery. My emotions, resignation, and disbelief still warred within me, making all of this feel like a terrible nightmare.

I actually stood at my brother Liam's grave as the rain pattered on the umbrella that protected me from the worst of the storm. Like a clip from a depressing movie. Around me, large trees with bloodred autumn leaves attempted to brighten the expanse of neat rows of headstones, but only added to the sense of death around me. Muted sunlight struggled through dark clouds, washing a gray morning landscape in a soft light that seemed almost surreal. The scents of rain and freshly cut grass made the world smell of life, which was painfully ironic.

All of it. All of it was painful, no matter how I tried to look at it.

Even the mist, which gave my city its name, was heavier

than usual. It appeared as nothing but mist to the humans of these lands, but the magical creatures saw it for it was. Ghosts. The spirits that walked the earth had all surfaced to mourn my brother's crossing over into their realm. Their soft sounds filled the air like a low, howling wind.

And yet, even though grief hung so thick in the air it was hard to swallow, I felt nothing.

Nothing at all.

I simply wanted to fade away into the empty shell that was now my body, but my instincts wouldn't allow it. I was aware of at least one person, if not more, breathing in the shadows of the trees. His, or her, heart racing.

And the person's focus was on me and me alone. I could sense a gaze trained on me so intently it was a physical sensation. A crawling that moved slowly down my spine.

This sort of situation is likely why my security team was so angry I sent them away.

No matter the day, there is always danger.

It was foolish to ignore a potential threat, I knew that. I might be as strong and quick as a vampire, but I no longer had the legendary powers that others had feared for so long. Here, alone, I had made myself vulnerable in a way my brother never would have when he was the ruler of our lands.

But I am not my perfect brother. As my people already know.

"He was a good person."

I stiffened as earth swirled together and took on the form of an old man. The excess dirt fell away and left an earth spirit with the coloring of the wet ground. His brown eyes were sad as he tilted his head to the side, watching me.

Even the creatures of ancient magic feel his loss. Most of the beings that could read minds and sense feelings left me unnerved. But the ancient spirits? They kept my secrets.

"Yes," I responded evenly. "He was."

My brother was my best friend. My protector. He handled the worst of our responsibilities as the leader of our clan. And he handled them *well*.

"He made life better for all of us," the earth spirit said, adding to my thoughts. He gestured to the rain. "Even the earth is crying for him."

"And he made it look so damn easy."

The old man chuckled. "That he did."

Liam alone had created a city where humans and magical beings lived in harmony. The creatures of the night were no longer predators, and the humans their prey. Even the most stringent of vampires either fed from the blood bank or from willing Feeders.

My brother enforced strict rules to keep the humans from discovering the truth, rules that kept fae, dwarves, and all magical beings safe from persecution. Mist was one of the few places in our world where most of the humans believed they lived in a town without supernatural creatures. If we didn't have such deep roots in Mist, we would have left a long time ago to the many other places in our world where humans were a protected species, almost extinct, and our people thrived. But our people were far too proud to ever do such a thing.

And then there was Liam's greatest accomplishment—harnessing the magic from the dead to create a glamour over our lands. It concealed magical beings, making them appear like normal humans. At least to the humans. The idea was pure and utter genius, and something that could only be done in Mist, because of the abnormal amount of ghosts.

My brother made this place a haven for all of us.

But now all of his responsibilities were mine alone. And

as easy as Liam had made it look, there was a reason that chaos had reigned before he took the throne.

And why Mist had been considered the most dangerous city in North America.

"I believe you will continue creating a better world for us all," the earth spirit said gravely.

I bowed my head, acknowledging the responsibility. "I will do my best."

Dirt swirled around him once more. "And though there are those that called him the light twin and you the dark, the earth has sensed in you more than death since the very beginning."

Like a powerful wind blasting a castle made of sand, the old man's shape scattered until nothing remained of him except his words. *More than death.*

What could he mean? Because my life has been circled by death ever since I was born. I couldn't fathom an answer that made sense.

I surveyed the rain-soaked ground. The lawn around the freshly dug grave had been churned by the sea of mourners who had long ago returned to Darkmore Manor. I kicked at a chunk of overturned grass with my nine-inch Valentino heels. Already dirt speckled the intricate lace design. My brother would have teased me for wearing the expensive shoes to such an event. He would have called them impractical, and then he would have bought me another pair to cheer me up.

Jerking my gaze away from my heels, I tried not to think of happier times. *Most of Mist, and every vampiric house around the country, is waiting for me. Why am I still standing here?*

But as much as my mind screamed for me to leave too, to graciously welcome the mourners into the home that was now my own, to comfort the many different races whom Liam had cared for so diligently, I simply couldn't leave. For reasons I couldn't understand.

The servants will take care of them, I thought, attempting to justify my actions. But in reality, I felt too spent to even imagine facing the mourners again.

I can't comfort them. Not when I'm so empty.

So hollow.

So numb.

They would expect emotion from me but I had nothing left to give.

In the days since my brother's murder, I'd cried more than I thought possible. Behind closed doors, alone in my room, I had vented the helpless grief and rage at what had been done to him. Liam, the light in a dark world, the person who made me believe in goodness, was gone. Never again would he tussle my hair. Never again would his booming laughter fill the quietness of Darkmore Manor. Never again would I know what it felt like to be entirely vulnerable with another person.

Do not forget it's all about perception, my love, he would tell me. *You are only as strong as they think you are. Make them believe it.*

My heart has died with him.

And so, I remained standing still, even as the hairs stood on the back of my neck. Even while the feeling of danger lurking in the shadows grew more intense.

Soon enough I would assume the role of Lady Darkmore, leader of one of the most powerful clans in the United States.

But for now, I was still just Dawn.

So for a little longer, I refused to let anything disturb me, including the person watching me from the shadows.

Yet, I can only delay going back for so long.

When I returned to Darkmore Manor, I would hold my head high and make them believe that I would be as fine a leader as every ruler in my family before me. I would make my brother proud.

I will leave the graveyard soon, I promised him silently. *The second I can imagine life without you by my side.*

But I couldn't imagine it.

I bowed my head. *Then again, perhaps I'll remain here forever.*

A tear escaped and trailed down my cheek. I reached up and touched it, numbly staring at the moisture. *I guess there was something left within me, after all.*

My ears caught the faintest sound of someone walking across the recently mowed grass behind me. Despite my misery, I tensed. Waiting.

If someone had decided this would be the moment to take down the heir to the clan, I would unleash every bit of fury inside of me and make them wish they'd never been born. My teeth gritted together, and my hands curled into fists.

The lone person approached closer and closer.

I narrowed my eyes and waited.

4

Dawn

A SECOND LATER, the woman's strong herbal scent came to me, and my shoulders relaxed. Damn. No one was going to pay today. My fury would have to remain bottled up for another day.

A slow poison. That's what my brother would call my anger. But, I didn't care. It was a poison I was gladly drinking.

"I'm sorry," Layla whispered. "I can't imagine how you must be feeling, how you can remain standing when the rest of Mist is so broken. As I walked here, the sounds of the dwarves' tools crafting creations for his grave echoed through the valley, and the howls of the inconsolable werewolves seemed to vibrate through me. And yet, their pain can't begin to compare with your own."

I took a deep breath that seemed to fill my whole chest and turned away from the elegant marble headstone to face the woman that had been my brother's advisor. And in another world, who could have been my friend. Layla wore a long black skirt and a long-sleeved blouse, so different from the Seer's usual colorful clothing. Her short auburn hair framed the gentle curves of her heart-shaped face, which her magic kept perfectly dry. As always, even as a Seer, she radiated a welcoming kindness that concealed her powerful talents from those who didn't know her well.

"Thank you," I said, although I longed to say more. To have one person to call my confidant or friend. Especially Layla. A woman I knew had a good heart and could be trusted.

But she will always keep that wall between us, just like the others. Fear is a powerful and illogical thing.

Layla moved closer, the tiny bells woven throughout her braided hair jingling with the movement. "I wanted to give you more time, but I simply can't."

I felt a flash of fear but quickly hid it away behind my customary emotionless mask. "Have you had a vision?"

Layla's visions were rare. But when they came...my brother always took heed. Because when ignored, her warnings had grave consequences. *Like for my parents.* A bitter laugh echoed through my mind. *How were they to know their only daughter would be the one to kill them?*

"Yes, I have. One that I haven't entirely made sense of, but I thought you could help untangle." Layla walked to my brother's headstone and knelt, her fingertips hovering over the simple inscription. *Lord Liam Darkmore. Loved by all.*

"And?" I held my breath.

Layla glanced up, her startling green eyes holding a wealth of unspoken emotion. "You will be challenged for your position as leader of the clan."

My breath came out in a rush. "Impossible! The Darkmore family has led our clan and ruled these lands for longer than the houses have existed."

And who would dare to challenge me? My thoughts raced through the other four leaders of the houses and immediately froze on one name. *Draven Cerberus.* The hairs on the back of my neck rose. There were houses that hadn't been pleased with the new restrictions my brother had implemented, but Draven always seemed to be silently seething, waiting for a moment to strike.

He's the one.

"There would have to be a vote. And a split in the votes of the four for a challenge to be made," I said, the pit in my stomach growing. *Since I can't vote for myself.*

Layla's gaze remained trained on the headstone. "There will be. And the vote will be split."

This can't be happening. Draven had fire Elementalist magic running through his blood.

I can't hope to defeat him. Not without my death magic.

Yellow lilies appeared in Layla's hand, and she bent and laid them gently on the bone-white marble headstone before standing to her full height. "The Darkmore family has ruled for so long because of the mix in their bloodlines. Having the magic of the fae and the abilities of vampires made your family almost invincible." Her tone gentled. "If you had your powers, none would be foolish enough to challenge you. But the leaders of the houses see you as weak. They have been waiting for an opportunity like this for centuries. There will be a grab for power soon. And if you lose, the humans and magical creatures in Mist will suffer unimaginably. You cannot lose."

"Those *ungrateful* wretches...after all my family has done for them." I felt hot. My umbrella tumbled from my fingertips, and within seconds, I was soaked. "This can't be. My brother," I choked on the words for a moment. "My brother has just died. I should be focused on keeping the peace my brother fought so hard for. Not on this...treachery."

"I am sorry," Layla said. She hesitated, reaching out as if to touch me, but then dropped her hand. "In my vision, if you stand alone against the odds, you lose."

"I...lose?" I couldn't swallow around the lump in her throat. The world seemed to tilt under my feet.

What would there be left for me then—if not to care for my people?

"If you stand alone," Layla emphasized, as if it mattered.

My long dark hair slid into my eyes, wet and cold. I pushed it back, overwhelmed by a desperation that fought to sweep me into absolute hopelessness. "But I *am* alone. Layla, don't you understand? Only Liam was truly ever there for me. Only he knew what it was like to be envied, hated, loved, or feared but never understood or seen. I *do* face my enemies alone."

For some reason, my thoughts turned to a boy standing in the rain, his eyes filled with hopelessness. Of another person who took away the sense of loneliness that ate at me night and day. I jerked, my heart pounding. *Why do I always think of him in moments like this? It's been years since I saw him last. It's pathetic.*

"Heavy is the head that bears the crown. I understand. You're always in the company of others, but you're always alone. It doesn't take my powers of sight to see that." Layla cautiously reached out and grasped my shoulders, holding my gaze. "But all is not lost. There was a man in my vision. When you are challenged to a battle for your position, you'll only win with him by your side."

I'll be challenged to a battle. And because of the loss of my powers, I'll have to appoint a champion to fight on my behalf.

The thought made bile rise in my throat. Never had a member of my family been so weak.

A hysterical laugh bubbled from my throat. "A man? What man?"

"This one." Tingles radiated from Layla's touch, and suddenly, I was swept into a vision.

Images flashed briefly. Of darkness. Of a man running for his life. Of a street filled with shops, and an alley. He stumbled down the alley, found it blocked, and turned back. But it was too late. Sharp teeth glinted and blood ran. A last gasp of breath shook his frame, and then he was still.

Without my help, he'll die.

I gasped, my thoughts scattering. I clung to every detail, striving to find clues as to the man and the place I might find him. At last, one of the shop names made me pause. I closed my eyes and pictured the street.

"I don't know who he is." I licked my dry lips. "But I know where he is...at least where he'll be soon."

A place I haven't been to in many years. Since I was young.

Opening my eyes, Layla's hopeful face came into view. "Where? Where will he be?"

I didn't hesitate. "Ghost Town, Arizona."

Layla released my shoulders and took a step back. "You have family there, right? Can you ask them for help?"

Great Aunt Lucilla, and a multitude of distant cousins. "Perhaps, but it's been a long time since I've seen her, and even then, she was a bit...eccentric."

"Well, it can't hurt to ask." Layla gave me a forced smile. "Especially when you're running against the clock."

I took a deep breath. "How much time do you think I have?"

Layla didn't hesitate. "In my vision, the battle takes place on the night of the eclipse."

That gives me less than a week...

Taking one last look at my brother's grave, I made a promise to myself and to him. I wouldn't lose Darkmore or destroy our family legacy. I would push aside my grieving, just as I had done when my parents died, and hide behind my persona.

Righteous anger surged through me then. *I have spent my whole life doing things for the good of our people. Carrying the weight of being a Darkmore, spending my days doing work for our kind. And the moment Liam is gone, they challenge me?*

I am Lady Dawn of Darkmore Manor. Draven and his ilk have no idea what I can do. From now on, no one will see my fear, or my grief. I will find this champion, and we will win. Then they will see a woman who can lead them. A woman who can protect them. A woman who will carry on the Darkmore legacy.

I snapped the umbrella shut, making my way swiftly to my car.

I have less than a week to save us all.

5

DRAVEN

I FROWNED as I watched Dawn walk away from the Seer. Flames danced in the center of my palm as I watched the Seer with her troublesome prophecies climb into her car. I couldn't hear what she had said to Dawn, but her prophecies had been far too accurate in the past.

This can't be good.

I had planned every single detail of my acquisition of the house of Darkmore. *And its Lady.* I would give Dawn a small amount of time to mourn her dead brother, enough time that other houses wouldn't find my actions *too* crass, and then I would challenge her as leader of the coven. There would be a vote, and as much as I had threatened and bribed the other vampires, the vote would be even.

Damn Jareth and Lorcan and their loyalty to a bunch of dead Darkmores. Everyone knows Dawn can't rule the Darkmore house alone. She needs a man by her side to lead.

Then, because there would be no clear winner, I would

propose the customary fight to the death. Dawn would know she had no chance of winning. She would be desperate. Then, privately, I would make her the offer. Take my hand in marriage, and save her life and her pride.

With no other option, she would agree.

My groin tightened at the thought. Beautiful Dawn. A woman who always seemed so untouchable. How many nights had I dreamed of sharing a bed with her? Of claiming her as my own?

I would have power, and I would have her. At last, I would be content.

And then, the real work would begin. I was tired of hiding who I was just to protect the humans of Mist. I was tired of the other magical beings thinking they were equal to vampires. *We have powers for a reason. And humans are our food. Lions are not friends with gazelles.*

A sneer tore from my lips. My reign would be one of chaos, blood, and power. The law of the jungle. As it always had been. As it was meant to be.

I followed Dawn in the shadows, watching as she climbed into her car and tore out of the parking lot. A minute later, a second car, driven by my werewolf Tracker made the slightest sound as it followed after her. I caught the faintest shimmer of sunlight reflecting off the metal of his invisible car, and then both vehicles disappeared from view.

Whatever she was planning, I'd know soon enough.

Nothing would stop me now.

Another car pulled into the parking lot. An older woman with white flowers stepped out, opening her umbrella. Even from a distance, I could smell the scent of her sweet blood.

I was tired of reheated blood in bags and the willing,

pathetic Feeders who allowed me to sink my teeth into them. I wanted to see the panic in a human's eyes. To smell their fear. To drink from them until the life left their body, and then tear their throat to shreds, just for the fun of it.

The old woman knelt at a grave, her back to me.

I smiled. Today would mark the end of peace in Mist. This woman would be the first to die. And after that, many, many more bodies would litter the ground.

The streets will run with blood.

My feet sank through the wet grass as I silently made my way to my first victim.

6

DAWN

MY MANOR WAS FILLED with mourners, but I wanted nothing to do with any of them. Still, the lady of the house was expected to do certain things, even today. And as much as I couldn't believe another vampire had hurt my brother, I knew it was possible. Not as likely as one of the asshole shifters deciding they were tired of the prince of the vampires controlling Mist and killing him, but possible. So, I forced myself to move through the people, accepting their condolences, and trying not to look like I suspected all of them of being involved.

One good thing, perhaps the only good thing, about being known for so long as having the power to kill with a touch, was that people avoided me. Even though my powers had been gone since the day I'd accidentally killed my parents.

Trama, my brother had said, had caused my natural abilities to be suppressed. He'd reassured me that one day I'd be the most dangerous vampire among us once more.

I'd never had the heart to tell him I'd be happier if I knew my powers would never return. Being in this strange place where my powers didn't work, but people still feared me, and I still feared myself, wasn't a good place to be either. But it was better than feeling like a rigged bomb.

Now, I felt like I didn't know what I was.

With my powers, I could keep myself and my people safe. With them, I'd be alone forever.

Lord Jareth Emrick was suddenly in front of me. His dark eyes, ringed by red, were filled with sadness, and his blond hair was uncharacteristically swept back in a formal way. He bowed low as he took my hand. "I'm so sorry for your loss."

I sounded robotic when I answered back. "Thank you for your kindness."

"And, I want to reassure you that my men and I are working hard to find his killer."

"Thank you," I responded, squeezing his hand.

Jareth was more than an acquaintance to me. Not quite a friend, but I didn't think he was capable of killing my brother, even if he wanted to. Which he didn't. Jareth had liked all my brother's new rules and restrictions. So, I mentally removed him from my list of suspects.

"It was probably a shifter," a woman sneered.

I turned to see Bacia Kyran in a criminally tight black dress, giant heels, and a face full of dark makeup. So, basically, looking like she always did, except her dark hair was put into a loose bun at the nape of her long neck. She, like Jareth, was the leader of one of the houses that my family ruled over. And she was a world-class bitch. Yeah, she was right, the tension between shifters and vampires was notorious, but Mist was different from most places in the world. All of us supernaturals were trying to avoid humans discovering us, so we often worked together. I didn't hold them any ill-will. So, I was about as certain that the shifters were responsible as I suspected that she could be.

"Perhaps it was the shifters," Jareth said, dropping my hand. "But we'll learn the truth when we get all the forensic reports back."

"Or we could just hunt the fuckers down and make them all pay! Send a message to all the supernaturals that the vampires of Mist will not bow down to them." Her fangs elongated as she spoke, and I could almost picture the saliva ready to pour from her mouth at just the thought of all the death and blood she could enjoy.

I shook my head. "There has been enough bloodshed."

Bacia opened her mouth to argue, but I heard Draven behind me instead. "Please, Bacia, be respectful. Lady Darkmore has already been through so much."

Yeah, right. Bacia had grown up alongside all of us. We all knew she wasn't capable of being empathetic, regardless of the situation.

The female vampire gave me a dirty look, then sauntered toward Draven, squeezing his arm. "Of course, my lord."

But his gaze was glued to me. "If you need any help as you adjust to ruling, I'd be more than--"

I lifted a hand to silence him. "I've been ruling at my brother's side for a long time. It'll be different to rule alone, but I'm more than capable of handling it."

He looked like he wanted to say more, but nodded. "Just so you know, I'm always here."

I thanked him and all but ran from the room. The rulers of

the various houses were necessary for our continued success in keeping the vampires in check. But with them, there was always a careful dance when we interacted. A chess game. My brother had been so good at handling them, but I wasn't ready for all of that yet. I just wanted to melt into the floor and be forgotten.

Except that I still needed to find this champion. And soon.

When I had made my rounds to all the people who were there to show their respects for my brother, I slipped up the stairs, wanting to get out of there and find my champion as quickly as possible. But at the top of the stairs, my brother's lover and partner sat. Tears ran down his face, and he had his knees drawn up to his chest. Even though technically he was close to my age, he looked younger than twenty-something.

Perhaps it was because he was human. Or perhaps because he was heartbroken, but I wanted to comfort him like he was a small child.

I sat down beside him.

After a minute, Brian dropped his head onto my shoulder. "I'm just going to miss him so much."

I swallowed around the lump in my throat. "Me too."

"Who would have hurt him? He was so loved."

My vision blurred with more tears. "I don't know, but I'm going to find out."

Then, I turned, so his head was forced off of my shoulder, and his pale brown eyes met mine. "But, I think, you may want to go visit your parents for a while."

"Why?"

I didn't know how to explain myself, so I opted for the truth. "Things are going to get a bit crazy here. I trust my people with a human in the house, but there's a lot of people I don't trust. I think you'd be safer somewhere else until this all gets settled."

For a second he looked like he might argue, but then he swept a hand through his long blond hair and nodded. "I'll go home, but you be careful, Dawn. Your parents dying stopped your powers. How do you know that your brother's death might not start them again?"

I didn't. I didn't know anything. "Thanks. I'll be careful."

We hugged, and then both of us headed to our rooms. Him to stay somewhere safe while a usurper tried to take my position, and me, to go find a mysterious stranger in a town I hadn't set foot in in years.

It was all just another crappy task in the life of a cursed woman.

7

AIDEN

I STUMBLED, and a soft hiss escaped my lips as my injured arm brushed the side of the brick building. For one long second, the world spun. Bile rose in the back of my throat as I fought the wave of pain that threatened to sweep me into unconsciousness.

But they were right behind me. If I slowed down, even for a second, I was dead. And if I died, I couldn't retrieve the communicator. They would continue their torture of innocent lives.

In my mind, I heard the screaming that echoed through the labs where I was tortured. *No matter the cost, I have to keep going. I have to stop them.*

Even though I couldn't feel my feet touching the ground, and I knew I walked slightly tilted, desperately trying to keep my balance, I kept moving. My shifter senses meant that my vision was better than a human's in the dark, but it was my sense of smell that flooded me. Because even from this distance, I could smell the pack of shape-shifting warlocks close behind. Other magical creatures might think they were nothing more than a pack of werewolves, but I knew better.

Tonight may just be the night they finally kill me.

As I slid along the glass window of an antiques shop, leaving a bloody smear behind, my limp became more pronounced. For two months I'd been running from this pack, trying to accomplish my mission. I'd killed half a dozen of them. But my wounds never had time to fully heal because I never had time to rest. They hunted me in the light and in the dark. They hunted me across state after state as I tried to get the digital map to give me a more specific location where the device was concealed.

It's taken me too long to figure out where to go.

That damn warlock technology never pinpointed an exact location until I crossed the boundary to Arizona. Then, it had landed on Ghost Town. Before that, I'd never even known Ghost Town, Arizona existed.

The shape-shifting warlocks might be determined to take my life, but unluckily for them, I was just as determined to live. Despite my broken arm. Despite the gashes on my face, arms, and legs. And despite the older broken bones and gashes that still ached when I moved.

All I need is one night to rest. To heal. Then, they could never catch me.

A howl seemed to vibrate through the air.

They're too close. And gaining on me.

I wanted to shift, but there wasn't time. And frankly, I wasn't sure I had the strength to complete the transformation. Unlike the warlocks, who could change shape in an instant, into any animal form they chose, my hybrid nature had only mastered one form—that of the wolf. And it was a longer and more painful transition.

Yet, they're so proud of their abomination. Their first human-warlock hybrid...at least the first to survive their experiments.

Well, technically, their second.

But if they get their way it will be back to just one.

Behind me, my keen ears picked up the sound of dozens of paws slapping against the pavement. Unfortunately, the scent of my blood would lead them straight to me.

Turning down an alley, I limped forward, glancing behind me even though it cost me a precious second. But when I turned back, I came face-to-face with the high fence that blocked me in. At any other time, I could easily scale it. I gritted my teeth. *But not tonight. Not when I'm this injured.*

I started back the way I'd come but paused.

Suddenly they were there. Beneath the yellow-tinted streetlight, a pack of at least a dozen warlock shapeshifters waited. Their lips were pulled back into snarls that sent goosebumps racing down my spine. The light glinted off their razor-sharp teeth as they slowly stalked toward me.

Backing up, I tried to think of any way out. Any way that tonight wouldn't end in my death. But the truth was a vicious, painful thing. There was no way out.

But the device must be activated. They cannot continue to create more human-warlock hybrids like me!

When my back hit the fence, I froze. Even though death was imminent, I was bound and determined to go down fighting. Even if I couldn't think of a more painful way to go than being torn apart by a pack of vicious warlocks.

Ten feet from me, the largest wolf shivered and shifted, slowly rising as a naked middle-aged man with jet-black hair. *Aghader's human form.* "Aiden, you bastard."

I clenched my teeth, my sarcastic response coming out before I could stop it. "Aghader, how's the eye?"

Aghader snarled, which only further emphasized the scars across one side of his face. And the hazy white eyeball that was all that remained of his ruined eye. "You will pay for that, and every other infraction you've made against us, traitor."

My blood dripped in a steady rhythm beneath my feet. "I'm sure I will, but I wonder how many more of you I'll take down before I go."

The wolves snarled around Aghader, their dark, multi-colored fur standing on end. "Come on, boy." Aghader took a step forward. "You can't possibly win against us. But I'll tell you what, if you give me the map, I'll make it quick."

He means he doesn't want me killing any more of them in my final battle.

I smirked, even though my head was spinning faster and faster. "Sorry, old man, no can do."

Aghader shook his head. "You never could just obey, could you?" His tone gentled, if only for a moment. "You could have been great. The fastest. The strongest. Our greatest experiment. But you had to have a—"

"A crisis of conscience?" I filled in, followed by a hollow laugh. "That's my downfall, Aghader. You might have made me into a monster, but no matter how hard you tried, you could never take away my humanity. And that's something you all lack."

Seeing their underground lab filled with pleading humans and dead bodies changed everything. It didn't matter that I was sure they'd kill me before I could help; I had to steal the map and escape. I had to find a way to stop their experimentation.

A curtain seemed to fall over Aghader's face. "And just as I always warned, it's going to be the death of you."

I need to survive. To save the others.

I spread my legs into a fighter's stance, even though the movement had my vision blackening for a precious second. "But you should know, I don't have the map anymore. I destroyed it."

Aghader stiffened. "You're lying."

"I'm not."

His one good eye blazed with anger. "But you know the device's location?"

"Yep. I guess if you kill me, you'll never know."

Aghader looked troubled for one brief moment before a smile curled his lips. "You heard him, boys. The goal is to make this painful. To disable him. And then we'll take him home and torture him until we learn the whereabouts of the communicator."

I tensed. *That didn't go the way I planned.*

The warlock shapeshifters prowled forward. Their fur seemed to absorb the light from around them, making them more creatures of nightmares rather than the werewolves they strove to mimic.

And then a dark shape leaped down from the top of the building, soundlessly falling into a crouch onto the pavement in front of me. The woman, because she clearly was one, turned and looked back at me over her shoulder.

My breath caught. She was the most beautiful creature I'd ever seen. Her high cheekbones were flushed, rosy against her pale skin. Dark, shapely brows arched over stunning hazel eyes. But her hair was almost pure white, with the exception of the bloodred streaks woven throughout it. She was such an odd mix of beautiful and surprising.

Even the warlocks chasing me stood frozen.

For one second, so short it was like a trick of the light,

she gave me a reassuring smile, her features gentling. It made her look younger. Familiar.

Dawn. I inhaled a breath. *After all these years, could it really be her?*

Then her full lips opened slightly, flashing her sharpened canines.

She's a vampire? That's just not possible!

Whether I felt attraction or fear, I couldn't be certain, but I was shocked. The town we'd grown up in, Mist, didn't allow non-humans within its borders. It was supposed to be a safe place for a race that was facing extinction. Dawn had grown up there with me, so there was no chance she had been a vampire then. So had she been forced into Turning by one? The thought made me sick. No, she had to still be human. Right?

But now, staring at Dawn, a woman who had gracefully leaped from a building and had the sharpened canines of a vampire, there was no doubt. My heart ached for her. Not only had something tragic been done to her, just like it had been done to me, but now she could never return to our home.

She rose from her crouched position with a fluidity that told me she was a creature of magic, even if her leap from the building hadn't. Before her, neither the wolves nor Aghader moved, but all continued to watch her with unspoken wonder. She was a beauty. An angel. Something delicate and graceful. Flawless splendor in a world filled with ugliness.

The white jumpsuit she wore barely reached her upper thighs, showing off her long, bare, shapely legs. She screamed of money and privilege, from her clothing to the way she held herself.

"Wolves." Her voice held a confidence that bordered on arrogance. "What seems to be the trouble here?"

Aghader's shoulder went back, his gaze sliding over her curves with a greediness that made me growl low in warning. "Nothing to concern you. Just dealing out a little punishment for a traitor."

"A traitor?" One eyebrow lifted but there was no surprise in her voice, only curiosity.

"Yes." Aghader's gaze darted from me to the woman, and I knew he would soon spin his lies. "He went wild, killing a half dozen wolves in his pack without provocation. But no need to fear him, we will deal with him here and now."

She looked back at me, and I tried to stand taller, even though the motion made my head spin again. "This creature killed *six* shifters?" Slowly, she walked toward me, her movements sensual. "He doesn't look like a vicious monster to me. Perhaps he just needs taming."

To my surprise, when she got close enough, she reached out a hand and stroked the dusting of a beard on my chin. Standing up on the tips of her black boots, she leaned in. Her scent, a sweet combination of rain and freshly cut grass, filled my nostrils. Her tongue licked the blood from my earlobe, and her voice came soft as the wind.

"Agree to be my champion, and I will save your life."

My eyes widened as a shudder racked my body. What had she said? Her champion? My mind worked quickly. With the wolves there was certain death. With this... vampire, there was a chance at life.

And I would do anything for Dawn, now or then.

"Agreed."

She moved back from me, pausing as her brows drew together as she gazed at my face. *Does she recognize me too?* Then, her expression changed into one of arrogance once more as she whirled around to face the pack of enraged animals behind her.

"What is the name of your pack?"

Aghader straightened. "The Shadow Keepers."

"A pack that I believe has territory on Lord Cerberus's lands. If I'm not mistaken. And I rarely am."

The warlock's lips pulled into a thin line. "It is...I'm sorry, I don't believe I caught *your* name."

She rested a hand on one hip, confidence oozing from her. "Me?" She huffed as if insulted. "I am Lady Dawn Darkmore of Mist."

I almost laughed at the shock I saw on their faces. *Who is she that these warlocks are scared of her? Lady...what had she said?* Of course, vampires had royalty. But everyone at school had always just called her Dawn. And yet, there *had* always been something about her.

Staring at her slender back as she faced them, my memories cast me back to nearly ten years ago when I'd been a sophomore attending Night High School in Mist. Dawn Darkmore had been the most popular girl in school. To most of the people there, she was a stunning, wealthy girl who entered every room as if she owned it. Whom even the teachers seemed to bow down to.

But to me? To me, she was the girl who changed everything in one night, even though we'd barely spoken before, or since.

Why does it feel like tonight will be another night like that—when her presence changes everything?

"Or if you don't recognize me by that name, perhaps you've heard of my other title. Lady of Death."

The name sent a ripple of fear through the group. The wolves lowered themselves to the ground, as if acknowledging her dominance. Even Aghader took several steps back, looking between her hands and her face in shock.

Lady of Death? Why do they call her that? I'd heard the name whispered once or twice, but never paid attention to what was said.

"Well, Miss Dawn," Aghader said, stumbling over his words as he awkwardly dropped his hands down to hide his nakedness. "This matter—"

"Lady Darkmore," she corrected.

He froze, then continued more slowly. "Lady Darkmore. This isn't a matter for the vampires."

She patted her hair, which was stunningly braided to frame her delicate features. "You're right that normally the discipline between wolf packs is none of a vampire's business."

Aghader visibly relaxed. "Thank you, ma'am. I mean, Lady Darkmore."

"Wait." She held up a perfectly manicured hand. "I said *normally*. But I believe in this case I must remind you of the rules. The Darkmores may not rule your territory, but our good friends the Cerberuses do, and we rule them. When they allowed you within their boundaries, it was with the understanding that you were never to infringe upon vampire matters."

"Like I said," Aghader emphasized, the wolves around watching the exchange with narrowed eyes. "This is not a vampire matter."

"Oh?" There was a smirk in her voice. "But it is, my dear. For what else could you call your attack on my champion?"

Aghader's one good eye widened. "Your what?"

"My champion." She turned and gave me a sweet smile. "I have claimed him as my own. And he is very, very important to me. More important than you could possibly imagine. Now, when I first entered this..." She looked around, wrinkling her nose in disgust. "...place, I had determined to make a request of your vampire lord to throw you from his lands, even though it would mean that your pack would no longer have a territory of their own. However, after listening to your reasons for this attack, I have determined that my champion behaved rather badly, and perhaps deserved the beating he received."

Aghader's mouth hung open. Every wolf was watching the beautiful vampire, glued to her as if there was nothing more important than what she might say next.

"But," she emphasized, her hips swinging slightly as she moved closer to me. "I have need of him now. So it is time for you to be on your way."

Aghader finally closed his mouth. "My lady, surely you must understand—"

She waved a hand. "I understand all that I care to."

Spinning on her heel, she marched back toward me and wound one arm around my waist as she placed my arm around her shoulders.

My blood instantly marred her flawless white jumpsuit. "Your clothes..."

She shook her head, responding, "It doesn't matter."

As she started to slowly pull me along, right into the pack of stunned wolves, every inch of my skin itched. It went against my instincts. I was relying on this woman's words, her skills to convince the wolves who wanted me dead not to hurt us. If I'd had any other choice, not even the hounds of hell could have made me walk straight into the center of the pack, letting them surround me. But I was smart enough to realize I *didn't* have another choice.

Aghader and the wolves parted at her approach. Aghader shooting far from her reach as if horrified.

Why do they fear her so much? I held my breath, trying not to smell the stench of bloodlust around me. As we passed through the line of werewolves to the other side, I exhaled in disbelief. *Could this actually work?*

When we had nearly reached the exit of the alley, Aghader's voice came low and filled with fury. "I heard a rumor about you."

She didn't pause. "I never did care for rumors."

Continuing at a casual pace, she led us down the street. Behind us, the pack followed more slowly. It took everything in me not to turn around and face them, hating keeping my back to the enemy so much that it was almost a physical pain.

"It's okay," she whispered. "Don't look back and don't slow."

And so, I didn't. She turned at the first block and led me down two more streets before finally pausing. On the side of the quiet road, a white Bentley was parked, looking ridiculously out of place in the small town. Before she pulled her keys from her pocket, I knew the car belonged to her. Even in high school, she'd driven an expensive sports car.

Then, Aghader spoke, shouting from a distance. "I heard your powers are gone."

I felt her body stiffen under my arm.

She opened my car door and helped me climb into the passenger seat before standing up tall and staring across the space to where the wolves waited. "I wonder if you're willing to bet your life on a rumor." Then, she smiled, flashing her sharp teeth. "Because rumors so often serve my purposes."

Aghader's good eye widened slightly. I didn't like the calculating look on his face.

Circling around, she climbed in and turned the engine on.

Although almost imperceptible, I heard her whisper, "Go slowly. Stay calm."

Is she bluffing? If she is, she's good at hiding it.

Her hands stayed at ten and two as she steered around the wolves and drove down the quiet streets of the town.

"So can you really kill with a touch?"

She took a long moment before she answered. "I haven't been able to use that power for a long time."

I wasn't sure if her words were reassuring, or scary.

"You're in bad shape," she said, in a matter-of-fact voice. "I've called some family for help, and I got us a little cabin just out of town. You can heal there, and then we need to get out of here first thing in the morning."

Not before I retrieve the communicator.

But I nodded and winced, remembering my wounds. I looked down at the cream-colored seats. "Damn it, I've got blood all over your car."

"It's just a car."

I stiffened as she spoke the same words she'd said so many years ago. "I've heard that before."

She turned and stared at me, her eyes wide as her gaze ran over me. "Aiden?"

8

*D*AWN

*T*WELVE YEARS AGO...

I LEFT *the Halloween party early. Humans and vampires alike, all were drunken messes, making out, and dancing like idiots. In quiet rooms, rebellious vampires fed on the defenseless teens. I knew from too many parties just like this one that the humans would feel euphoria as they were fed upon. The vampires' arousal would grow out of control, and soon they would be feeding and having sex, as long as the humans were willing.*

And the next day? The humans would feel weak and confused, with only foggy memories of the night, and no memories of being used by a supernatural being.

The idea of what happened at these parties bothered me. Even though my parents emphasized that it was "normal." "It's what humans were created for, my dear." Her mother would say, shaking her head at the daughter she would never understand.

I was so tired of nights like this, but as my parents reminded me, I had an image to maintain. Not just as a normal sixteen-year-old girl among the humans, but also the vampires. They needed to cultivate a sense of both equality and superiority among their kind. "Power," my mother always said, "is half perception."

But I didn't want to go home yet. Not to my mansion full of people and my parents full of questions. So, I drove through the pouring rain, lost in thought. Listening to the sounds of the rain falling and my favorite song. The woman's voice poured out of my radio, a haunting melody that sent goosebumps prickling across my skin as I sang about how impossible it was to capture the past.

When the song ended, I blinked back into awareness. Somehow I had driven to the wrong end of town. And even though there was no reason for it, I turned down the road with its crowded trailers. The lights lining the street were dark, and the pavement under my tires, rough and cracked, sent me bouncing along.

As if compelled by a greater force, I turned down the street where his *trailer was parked.*

I must be a glutton for punishment.

There, standing on the sidewalk, was Aiden. And even though the rain, I knew something was wrong.

It went against everything I'd told myself. Even though I like him, I can't bring him into this. I must protect him from the dangers of my world.

No matter how much my heart told me he might be **the one.** *The love of my life.*

I promised myself as I headed toward him that I wouldn't stop, yet I was already slowing. I pulled up alongside him, put the car in Park, and threw open the door.

He glanced up, then turned around, hunching over. His back was to me.

"Aiden!" Racing to him, I tried to pull his shoulder so he faced me, but he held himself rigid.

I circled in front of him and finally got a good look at his face, then froze in shock.

He was a battered mess. One eye was so swollen it no longer opened. Blood ran from a cut in his forehead. His clothes were torn, sopping from the rain, and more blood leaked from his wounds. He's not one of us. These wounds could have killed him if they were worse.

I reached up to push his dark, wet hair from his face. He jerked, his uninjured eye focusing on my face. It was full of tears. Tears and the rain that ran down his face.

Tears prickled the back of my eyes. "What did he do to you?"

He dropped his head on my shoulder. His entire body shook, and I held him as he cried.

For too long, we stood in the rain together. I could feel his pain, every terrible moment he'd lived through to get to this point. I realized that the tall, thin boy who slouched as he walked around school had an even thicker wall between him and the rest of the world than I did. And tonight, that wall had finally broken.

At last, his shaking slowed. I led him to my passenger door and put him in. "I'll be right back."

He didn't move, as if he didn't hear me, so I shut the door.

A chill ran down my spine as every hair on my body stood on end. I turned ever-so-slowly to the trailer that his abusive foster father lived in. You like to hurt those that are weaker than you?

Perhaps so do I. Let's find out together, shall we?

As a child who could kill with a touch, I was no stranger to death. But this was the first time I wanted to kill. The first time I wanted someone to suffer.

Every step I took felt loud and heavy as I walked through the overly tall grass and up the steps. I wondered if inside the human could sense a predator in his midst. A light went on. The squeaky door opened as I stood in front of it.

"You back for more, you little bastard..." his words trailed off as his gaze fell on me. "Well, aren't you a cute little thing."

I pushed him back into the trailer.

Nearly twenty minutes later, I came back out and climbed into my car. I stared at my knuckles on the steering wheel. They were covered in blood. I felt nothing except satisfaction as I thought of the damage it took to break my immortal skin. Yes, I could kill with a touch, but this man did not deserve a quick death. He deserved the inhuman strength of a vampire.

"I got blood all over your car," Aiden said, his gaze unfocused as he stared at the dashboard in front of him.

"It's just a car," I said, then shifted into Drive. "I'm taking you to the hospital."

"No!" For the first time, he seemed to be aware of what was happening. "He won't like that."

I slowed, stopping at a stop sign. "You don't ever have to be afraid of him again. Do you understand? Never again."

I BLINKED as the past faded away. "Aiden, is it really you?"

He nodded, looking away from me.

For the first time in longer than I could remember, I felt anxious and uncertain. This was the boy who had influenced my life in ways he probably never realized. Who disappeared our senior year, never to return.

Until now.

We weren't really friends. Or close. It made no sense how hurt I was. How heartbroken.

"You look so different." Massive. He'd been tall in high

school, but now he was well over six feet. His shoulders were so broad they seemed to fill up the entire space, and with his gray shirt clinging to his muscular arms and chest, he looked like a bodybuilder. Even bigger than any shifter I'd seen before. "Is that what happened? You became a shifter?"

He didn't answer.

I was shocked by the wave of hurt his silence brought. *I don't know him anymore. And he obviously didn't feel the same about me, or he would have returned before now.*

Exiting the town, I tried to focus on the landscape beneath the bright moon's light. Ghost Town, Arizona was so different from Mist. Desert spread out in all directions, speckled with sick-looking trees and cacti. Everything was thirsty, dry, and dead. Even the air was parched.

At any other time in my life I might have thought it was beautiful and unique, but tonight, I missed the sense of green-life that filled the air in Mist.

But don't worry, Dawn. Soon you'll be back. To face your people and the challenge that might destroy us all. My hands tightened on the steering wheel. We'd be back, soon enough.

9

Dawn

TWENTY MINUTES LATER, we pulled off one road, and bounced down a couple more. On the side of a massive mountain of red rock, a cabin sat nestled at the base. I didn't know who it belonged to, only that a call to Great Aunt Lucilla had directed me to come here.

The lights in the cabin were on as we pulled up and I cut the engine.

"Do you have company?" he asked, his tone emotionless.

I stared at the brightly lit cabin, frowning. "I guess so."

Going around to his door, I prepared to help him. Instead, he climbed out slowly and kept out of my reach, hobbling toward the door.

Tearing my gaze from him, I grabbed my travel bag and medical kit from the trunk and followed him. The first thing I smelled was food cooking, and then I felt the sense of overwhelming warmth, along with the fact that every light seemed to be turned on in the house.

The one-room cabin was about the size of my bedroom back at my mansion. A sitting area with a blazing fire was on one side. A tiny kitchen table was just a few steps in front of them, and a wall filled with knick-knacks concealed my view of the kitchen. Most of the back of the room was taken up by a huge bed.

Lucilla came around the corner, drying her hands on a towel. "Finally, you're here!" She looked shockingly younger than I had imagined she would after so many years. Wearing a pretty purple blouse that somehow made her pale brown eyes stand out, with turquoise jewelry around her neck and wrists. In all ways, she looked ready to entertain, even though after taking one look at us she should have realized that wasn't the kind of evening we had planned for. She pushed hair streaked with blue behind one ear, grinned, and headed straight for me.

I thought I was prepared for anything, but my great-aunt took me completely by surprise. Lucilla didn't keep a safe distance; instead, she pulled me into a warm, friendly hug full of energy.

She hugged me? Just like that? I couldn't remember the last time someone had touched me so freely. *No, I do remember. It was Liam.* Just thinking about my brother made me stiffen and pull away.

"Sorry we're a bit late," I answered, feeling uncertain as the older woman smiled back at me. "The drive took longer than I thought."

An older man came around the corner with a frown on his lips and a coffee in his hand. He was Native American, with long dark hair streaked with white, and dark eyes. He wore a black uniform that seemed to be a size too small. But for all that, he also had a calmness to his persona that I instantly liked. "It seems there's been a bit of a disturbance in town. Lucilla thought I'd better ask you about it."

Lucilla patted his shoulder. "Officer Paul was going to come to your rescue, but I thought it better if you handled it yourself." The older woman winked, looking from me to Aiden.

I glanced at Aiden, feeling strangely flustered. There was a pallor to his skin that was so white it was nearly green. *He isn't going to be able to keep standing for long.*

"Why don't you take a shower?" I offered him, knowing he probably wanted some privacy. "And I'll handle...I'll stay out here."

His gaze went to the police officer, and Aiden got a weird look on his face, then did this strange sniffing thing.

To my surprise, the other man did the same thing.

I lifted a brow and looked between them. What were they doing? They looked like two dogs trying to sniff each other's butts. Which would've been funny to witness at any other time, but right now I was just exhausted and wanted to get through this whole family reunion thing.

"So, shower?" I asked Aiden, making a mental note to ask him about this whole thing later.

Aiden slowly nodded and shuffled toward the tiny bathroom tucked in the corner beside the bed, but not before shooting the other one last suspicious look. I tore my gaze from his back and attempted a smile for Lucilla, who surprised me by pulling me into a second hug.

I stiffened again, and Lucilla said, "Honey, you look like you need all the hugs you can get." Then, she pulled back and gestured to the table. "Now, take a seat, tell us all about it."

Reluctantly, I sat down at the little circular table with its four wooden chairs. The police officer dropped a coffee in front of me, then sat down, leaning back and sipping his drink. Lucilla sat beside him, watching me with a slight twinkle in her eyes.

I searched for words, unsure where to begin. I had spoken in front of far more people. I was used to high-stress situations that called for diplomacy. But for some reason, the openness of these people made me nervous. Lucilla radiated the energy of someone who knew me well and liked me, but the last time I'd seen my great-aunt had been more than twenty years ago. And the old police officer watched me with the judgment and understanding of a grandfather, even though I'd never met him before.

It was very, very unnerving.

"Well..." I cleared my throat. "It seems Aiden's pack was hunting him, for some reason. I convinced them to let him go. I don't believe there will be any more trouble in your town, Officer."

He snorted. "That's highly unlikely."

Lucilla smiled and her brown eyes sparkled. "I know all of that, sweetie. I mean, tell me about what's been going on with you."

I opened my mouth but felt completely at a loss for words.

The older woman reached out and squeezed my arm. Just the fact that someone touched me so easily, and without fear, only added to my confusion. *I never realized how isolated I've become. Since my parents died, I haven't touched anyone except Liam.*

"I've been thinking of you since that big rebellion, the one that killed your parents. It was an enormous loss, a whole generation of vampires killed off throughout Mist, leaving all you young kids to pick up the pieces."

This I could talk about. "Liam was incredible. He didn't

just stop the war between all the supernaturals; he convinced them that he could create a better Mist. That the vampires didn't have to be seen as the superior race any longer, that we could all live as equals, still under the noses of the humans."

Lucilla frowned, tilting her head. "Your brother did a great job, but you were the one that amazed me. You endured the worst trauma a child could imagine—having your gifts become a curse."

I started, my jaw working, overcome with emotion. "I didn't...I couldn't control..."

"I know, sweetheart. I know. Most creatures with supernatural abilities aren't able to control them when they are young. It's unfortunate that yours were so potent."

I swallowed around the lump in my throat. "Yes, *unfortunate*."

Unfortunate didn't begin to capture the horror of what I'd done, but then, no word really could.

"You know, your parents were well aware of the risk you posed. That's why they raised you and your brother to be such amazing leaders. To be so competent in their absence." She leaned closer. "They live on, through you. And they were so proud of you."

Although I hadn't believed it was possible, tears sprang to my eyes. "I...I find that hard to believe. And besides, Liam was the leader, not me."

"You shouldn't find any of this hard to believe. Never doubt the love they had for you. And don't underestimate the role you played in helping Liam build Mist into what it is today. You held your head high and faced the angry masses..."

"The fact that he was healing and protecting all of them made our people easier to face," I said, feeling defensive.

The light twin and the dark, the one that heals and the one that kills.

"I remember you as a child. Your vision of the future. You laid out the plans to create a better world in Mist, not your brother. He might have implemented them. He might have been the 'face' of the Darkmore house, but you were the dream behind it, essential to it all, and don't you forget it!"

I didn't want to hear any more. Old wounds were opening, cracking, and bleeding. I couldn't handle much more talk of the past when my emotions were already so raw about the present. "Thank you. But, uh, I'm actually here to bring a champion home, because the other houses believe that without my magic I'm not worthy of leading the clan. I'll be challenged, and being so weak without my powers, I'll lose without him." I paused, realizing how angry and bitter I sounded. *That's new.*

The officer sat up, sympathy gentling his face. "Great leaders become great only through facing great challenges. Remember that."

Or they lose and never become a leader at all. I shook the thought from my head. No matter what I had to do, too many lives were counting on me succeeding for me to lose.

I heard the slightest sound and looked up to see Aiden hovering in the darkness of the doorway to the bathroom. When our eyes met, he stiffened and came out. He wore nothing but a towel, and I gasped as I took in the sight of the many, many wounds on his chest, some older and some newer.

I'd risen from my chair before I realized what I was doing and rushed toward him. He stared at me, openly watching my every move.

"You need medical attention."

"I'm not human now," he growled. "I'll heal."

My lips drew into a thin line. "Yes, you'll heal, badly and with more scars unless you care for your wounds properly. Surely your pack knew this? Even vampires receive treatment after we're hurt."

He shrugged. "They were busy trying to kill me, remember? Besides, they weren't big on stuff like that."

The chairs squealed as the two older people rose behind them.

Paul grabbed a bag of stuff off the counter. "Sounds like my cue to leave." He started toward the door but spoke over his shoulder. "I made you both a batch of my famous chili. Cooked it myself."

"Don't worry, I helped," Lucilla added with a wink.

Paul glared back at her. "I can cook chili all by myself! Do it all the time," he grumbled, shoving his bag under his arm.

"Before you go," Aiden began, seemingly unaware of their squabble. "I'm looking for something in Ghost Town. Something I lost a long time ago."

He never mentioned needing to find anything. My stomach tightened. *I hope it doesn't take long. I need to get home.*

Lucilla tapped her lip. "If you need some help, ask for a fairy named Sabrina at the post office. Her specialty is finding lost things."

He grunted a thank you.

A fairy? A fairy I could handle. They were much better than most of the fae. Fae were more powerful in a lot of ways, but they were similar to vampires in that they were often rich and elusive. They wanted little to do with humans, or even other races, and saw themselves as better than all other races. Fairies, on the other hand, usually liked to be of help and weren't nearly as stuck up.

Paul put his hand on the doorknob. "You coming?"

But Lucilla didn't follow him, instead, she walked right up to Aiden and grinned. "Boy, you are a handsome thing…a little rough around the edges, but I think you'll suit my Dawn just fine."

I blushed. "Aunt Lucilla, we're not—"

"Maybe not yet," the older woman grinned. "But soon. And, man, is it going to be an explosion when you two finally—"

"Aunt Lucilla!"

The older woman threw back her head and laughed. "All right, I'll stop. And remember, if you need help again, don't call me. This is something I know you two will be able to handle on your own." Her expression grew more serious. "You *need* to handle on your own."

Had she seen a vision of the future? Or had someone told her one? It was the only way to explain her words. My aunt was a woman who loved to help her family, after all.

Lucilla headed for the door and the police officer opened it, shaking his head.

"Have a nice night!" She called over her shoulder, looking back at us and winking. And then, she pulled something out of the pocket of her dress and placed it on the top of my medical kit. "And I had a friend make this for his wounds. It's a disinfectant, you know, without all that nasty burning."

"But how did you—?" I began.

"The Fates, of course." Her smile widened. "Make sure you rub it on him real slowly. It'll help with his sore muscles and repair broken bones too. It's really some good stuff. Just be sure to cover *every* inch of him in it." Then, she winked again and walked out the door.

Oh boy, now what am I in for?

10

DAWN

I CLOSED my dropped jaw and went to the door, turning the locks slowly to secure it after us. Putting off the moment I'd have to face him. As the last lock turned, I nibbled my lip and turned back to him. "Have a seat on the couch. I'll get my medical kit."

"Like I said, I don't need it."

Impertinence I could deal with.

Raising my chin, I gave my most arrogant look. "And how exactly are you going to be my champion when you're a wounded mess? Sit down and stop being a pain in the ass."

His intense blue eyes locked on me, and for a minute I thought he might argue, but instead, he went to the couch in front of the fire and gingerly lowered himself onto the edge.

For a minute, I could scarcely breathe. He was so ridiculously gorgeous. Dark hair. A scruff of a beard, and muscles for miles. And the fact that he was in nothing but a towel? It was downright criminal.

He caught my gaze. "I don't suppose they could have left me some clothes…"

"I'm not sure my aunt is your size," I joked, going to the table by the door and picking up the medical kit and special disinfectant.

"I meant the police officer," he muttered, and I couldn't help but grin.

I hurried back to him, but slowed my pace as I got closer to the couch and sat down beside him. Opening the kit, I laid out the familiar items, then hesitantly reached for the white cream my aunt had left me in a silver tube without markings.

How many times did I patch up Liam after a bad fight? And how many times did Mom tell me never to leave home without my kit? A smile came and went in an instant. *Don't think of your family now.*

I squeezed the magical vanilla-scented cream onto my palm, then turned to face Aiden and froze. Forgetting to breathe. My heart skipped a beat. Even closer, he was impossibly big. And impossibly handsome. But at least he wasn't looking at me. He was looking down at my hands.

"What is that?" He nodded at the cream.

"Something that should help you heal faster. Okay?"

He shrugged. As I concentrated on the extent of his injuries, my stomach turned. *I can't believe he survived this.* After a minute, I realized I was holding my breath.

Remembering to breathe, I inhaled sharply and studied his wounds. There were claw and teeth marks covering almost every inch of him. Some were badly healed, others looked infected, and still others were fresh. *The wolves.* But then there were other marks…unexplainable ones. They looked like careful incisions that had been left open to heal without help.

As if a torturous surgeon had played with him. For years.

I shivered. "How did you get that scar?" I asked, pointing at one.

He glanced down, then jerked his head back up. His mouth pulled into a thin line, but no words came out.

Fine. Don't tell the woman that saved your life.

I was angry as I reached my hand out and began to apply the cream over his chest, arms, and stomach. But even still, I was gentle. As irritating as I found his behavior, it was clear he'd already had a lifetime of pain. I had no intention of adding to it unnecessarily.

Again, an image flashed in my mind of him as a teenage boy as I walked past him in school. My crowd of loud, confident girls chatted around me like a whirlwind. He would glance up from his locker, his back curved into a hunch, the tattered hood of his sweater pulled up. The look of loneliness and longing that filled his expression made the world around me fade away. The expression that he hid so poorly reflected exactly the way I felt on the inside.

Had I been anyone else, had he not been an innocent human, I would have run from my group and wrapped my arms around him. Because in his eyes I saw the promise of something amazing—a kindred spirit. An end to my endless loneliness.

I shook my head and glanced down. My hand had stopped moving on his stomach, touching the hard planes. How long had I been lost in thought, touching him so intimately?

His eyes were closed, a pained look on his face.

Stop ogling him right now, look at how injured he is!

Squirting more of the cream onto my hands, I knelt between the fireplace and the couch. I rubbed the wounds on his legs as gently and thoroughly as I could. When I pushed back his towel ever so slowly and began to rub the claw marks on his inner thighs, he groaned.

I withdrew my hands. "Did I hurt you?"

His eyes were still closed, his whole chest moved with his rapid breathing. "Yes. But—thank you."

I rose and went to the sink, washing the blood from my hands. When I came back, I pulled butterfly Band-Aids from my kit. *I hope there's enough.*

But then, there's probably enough in this massive specialty kit to patch up an army.

The white bandages were perfect for any creature that healed quickly. Using the small, white strip, all I had to do was pull wounds closed and place the strip in place to hold the sides together. The vast majority of the time, within a few hours, the wound had closed with the help of the bandages. After a few days, there would be no scar remaining at all.

His eyes finally opened and a frown tugged at his lips. "What are those for?"

"The worst of your wounds. If we use these, you'll heal faster and without scars."

He huffed, a sound that was almost an angry laugh. "We wouldn't want me to scar."

I glared at him as I gently pulled the skin of his wounds together and placed the Band-Aids on. "You don't have to act like such an ass. I'm only trying to help."

When he didn't answer, my anger went up a notch.

"What happened to you? You used to be so nice in high school."

He stiffened beneath my touch, and I immediately regretted my words. It'd been a long few days. I was emotionally raw before I realized that my champion was someone I had such complicated feelings toward. But that was no excuse for my behavior.

He spoke before I had a chance to apologize. "I'm sorry. I'm not trying to act like an ass." He rubbed his face and then ran his hand through his dark hair. "It's just been so long since...since someone was...gentle with me."

If I'd felt bad before, now I felt worse. "I'm sorry too. I shouldn't have said that. You're just not saying much. Even that stuff about needing to find something in Ghost Town, what's that about?"

His deep blue eyes flickered to me, his gaze intense.

I looked away, uncertainty fluttering in my stomach as I placed the last Band-Aid on his legs. Then, I reached for wound dressings for the spots that still bled. *For a shifter to still be bleeding after this long, he must have been in pretty bad shape before tonight.*

"You said you needed a champion."

I nodded, not wanting to talk about it, but knowing I had to tell him. "In less than a week, I'll be challenged for my position as clan leader in Mist. I can either fight my enemy or appoint a champion. A Seer prophesied that I could only win with you as my champion, so I came for you."

And because of my loss of magic, I'm too weak to do it on my own.

It took him a long minute to answer. "You need me to fight a vampire for you?"

My cheeks heated. "He isn't just a vampire. He's a fire elementalist." *He's dangerous.* Something cold slid through my veins. *Don't say it.* But I had to. "I know you agreed to be my champion to get out of a bad situation. If you don't want to, now that you know more—"

"No," he said without hesitation. "I'm not backing out. But there's something I need to do first."

I repeated his earlier words. "Yes, find something in Ghost Town."

Securing the last of the dressing on his legs, I stood up and sat on the edge of the couch to reach the rest of him. My gaze ran over his many, many wounds. *Where to start?* I reached for the butterfly Band-Aids, focused on his massive shoulder and forearm.

"The Shadow Keepers are not shifters."

I stiffened and waited, focusing on my task, giving him time to work out his words. *Just like when we were young.*

"They're warlocks."

Warlocks is he serious? Warlocks aren't real.

"They're actually shape-shifting warlocks from another realm."

*Another realm? I'm pretty sure we'd know if there were other realms...*But I keep my thoughts to myself.

When I said nothing, he continued, sounding a bit more confident. "I know how crazy that sounds. All you magical beings seem to think vampires, fae, and shifters make perfect sense. But believing in warlocks? Just insane."

I smiled because he seemed so relieved that I was listening to him.

"The problem isn't that they're warlocks. The problem is that they're bad warlocks. Criminals hiding out in our realm. And their only ticket out of this realm is successfully creating a human-shifter hybrid, and then letting their superiors know...at least that's what they've been banking on."

"Okay." I hesitated. *Do I believe him about the warlocks?* The answer came quickly. *As ridiculous as the notion sounds, I do.* Because I trusted him. I always had. "So what do they want with human hybrids?"

He shrugged. "I've heard mixed things. Their boss either

plans to sell the hybrids or use them in some scheme of his. I guess their people have been having some issues with a declining population, and they haven't successfully found another race to breed with, so this was the next best thing. Either way, he said that if they can't get the job done, they can rot here."

I turned this new information over in my mind. "Okay. And what does this have to do with what you need to find?"

He took a deep breath. "They've successfully created a hybrid, so all they need to do is contact their superiors, and they've got a ticket out of this realm."

"Isn't that a good thing?"

His expression tightened, his eyes going distant. "No. Because once they learn that humans can be altered, they're going to expand their operations. Make a lot more hybrids to increase their progeny. And then, none of mankind will be safe."

I stared, letting his words sink in. So there was a group of criminal warlocks who were experimenting on humans and if they let their superiors know, all of mankind would be in danger? That was bad. Not end-of-the-world bad, especially with human numbers already so low, but bad enough. "So you're trying to stop this?"

He nodded. "And the only way to do that is to find the communications device before they do. I've seen them use it in the lab. If I'm lucky, I can talk to the right warlocks, and send these bastards home."

I let the breath I didn't know I was holding out. *This is unbelievable.*

But I guess no less unbelievable than the fact that I'm a vampire.

"So what happens if we don't stop them?"

"More people will be turned into freaks." Another pause.

"Freaks like me. And, honestly, I think this might finally be the thing to wipe out the human race altogether."

I stared, and for the first time, everything came together. *Aiden isn't a shifter. He's some kind of warlock experiment?*

"How are you...different from them? From shifters?"

His brows drew together. "The only thing I have in common with those...warlocks is on a biological level. I can shift, but only into wolf form. The other shapes that they changed into weren't of our world, so for whatever reason, I couldn't mimic them. But beyond biology, I'm nothing like them." He was breathing faster and faster, his muscles tensing. "If you saw all their 'failed experiments' you might understand why I don't like to be associated with them. And as far as how I'm different from a wolf shifter, I'm not really sure. But I am. The shifters I've met said I smelled bad. Wrong. They wanted nothing to do with me."

"Have you tried reaching out to the Human Defenders? I have an old friend from Mist who became one. I could reach out to her."

He shook his head. "I've heard the warlocks talk about them. They have people on the inside, so they're not safe to reach out to."

"Sammi wouldn't be in anyone's pocket," I told him, knowing without a doubt that she'd do anything to protect a human. She might be human herself, but she was one of a kind.

"I can't risk the fate of humanity on someone you knew when you were little," he said, not meeting my gaze. "Time changes everyone."

"Okay," I agreed, even though I felt like a special force dedicated to saving humans would be a strong ally for us, and continued carefully dressing his wounds.

Which brought me to the next thing that had been bothering me. *How have they been able to do all of this without anyone knowing? Without* me *knowing?*

Anger raced through me, followed by a horrible realization. "The Shadow Keepers' home is on Draven Cerberus's lands—in Mist. Is it possible he's aware of what's going on?"

Aiden slowly shook his head. "I don't know who that is or who they were involved with on the outside. They wouldn't have trusted me with information like that."

"I can't believe you were being tortured right under my nose!" I hit the back of the couch with my fist. "The Shadow Keepers were given permission to use lands, under the belief that they were a pack of shifters without a home of their own. They would have needed to talk to a man I know in length to do so. Did you ever see them with a vampire with silver hair and orange-and-red eyes?"

He frowned. "Dawn, I was their first 'successful' experiment. They hunted me like an animal to test my skills. They pretended I was 'one of the pack,' but someone was always watching. It wasn't until right before I left I even knew that they were experimenting on other humans. And that I found out by accident." He got quiet. "Then I realized the whole underground of our base was a lab. Or better yet, a massive torture chamber of screaming humans and dead bodies."

The guilt I felt was overwhelming. But did Aiden realize my role in all of this? Probably not. Or he wouldn't be talking to me right now.

I couldn't breathe as I forced out my confession. "My family rules over those lands."

He frowned, looking confused. "What do you mean?"

"My family rules over four other powerful vampire houses, as well as our own, of course. Draven Cerberus answers to us. We should have known what was happening on those lands. Especially if it involved magic...or warlocks...or shifters, for that matter."

He watched me carefully for a long minute, then seemed to come to some kind of decision. "None of that matters now, it's all in the past. What matters is the future."

It matters to me. There's no way Draven is going to get away with torturing humans on my lands. His house will go down for this.

I gritted my teeth. "Of course. We'll deal with your warlocks, and then we'll deal with my traitor."

I slowly began to tend to his wounds again, but in my mind, I'd come to a realization, for the first time I was glad Draven planned to challenge me to a fight to the death. Because I suspected his involvement with the warlocks, and for such a crime, his life was forfeit. Even though our coven was powerful, no one could break the rules involving humans. With their numbers so low, the government would come down on these people hard.

Except that we couldn't tell them, because Mist was supposed to be a human-only town. Which meant I was the law on those lands, and I would have to execute justice to the people who had hurt Aiden. Something I was more than happy to do.

My thoughts swirled. If I had my powers, things would be so simple. Killing Draven and destroying the creatures that had hurt Aiden would take no effort...no effort at all. Except that just the thought of having my powers back made me feel sick.

I kept telling myself how much easier life would be with my gift, but deep down I thought I would be happier without it. I was terrified that my curse would take the life of another person I loved. Even when my brother was killed, my head longed to discover his murderer and bring him or her to justice, but my heart never truly wanted that.

My heart...it never wanted to experience death in any form again.

Yet, now, thinking of Draven, a man who thought to usurp my throne before I even had time to grieve my brother. A man who had "failed" to notice the warlock shifters and their activities on his lands...maybe, just maybe, he deserved to die.

Yet, could I ever truly take a life again?

I looked down at my hands.

Inside, my magic stayed silent, an answer that was louder than any answer I could scream.

11

AIDEN

I DIDN'T KNOW which part of my situation was more unbelievable. The fact that Dawn Darkmore, the only girl I'd ever loved, was touching me, or that she was a vampire. *When I knew her in high school, I thought creatures like her were awful human-eating monsters forbidden from our lands.* What was more, I had told her about the existence of warlocks, and she wasn't laughing in my face.

Whatever the reason, I was overwhelmed with gratitude.

Her small, soft hands continued to brush my skin as she placed the bandages, moving to the wounds on my chest. Yes, I hurt, but pain was something I was used to. The feel of her hands on my body? Not so much.

Her touch. Her concern for me. I could barely remember to breathe. I was overwhelmed by her presence.

Is it just that I'm her champion? Or could she actually care for me?

As she closed my flesh, placing the pointless Band-Aids

on my skin, I tried to be subtle as I watched her. She was the most stunning creature I'd ever laid eyes on. Her hair was such a pale blonde color, that it was nearly pure white. Except, of course, for the places she'd died it a blood-red color. On anyone else it might have looked out-of-place paired with her heeled boots and white jumper, but it all just...seemed to work. Hell, she could probably dye her hair orange and still look both sophisticated and flawless in every outfit. She always had been like this though. Even in high school.

In the alley, she'd seemed like a hallucination. But here and now, she felt real...which was even stranger. How could a woman like her actually exist?

Years spent tied to a table, experimented on, trapped in rooms where my abilities were tested to their limits, I'd thought of her. In the back of my mind, I always believed that I had placed her on a pedestal. That no one could truly be as perfect as I imagined her to be.

But here she is, proving that I was wrong.

A shiver ran through me.

She looked up, her eyes, a light brown ringed by both green and blue, took my breath away. In high school, she had called them hazel. *But hazel could never describe eyes of such beauty.* "Did I hurt you?"

How could I tell her? How could she possibly understand how badly I craved her? I wanted to beg her to keep touching me. To touch me forever. Despite how weary I was...a bone-deep weariness that blackened the edges of my vision, my hybrid shifter blood wanted to claim her. I wanted to pull her to the bed, remove the bloodstained clothes from her body, and lay her beneath me and meld our bodies together.

I would please her because nothing would make me

happier. I would kiss her pale pink lips and taste her to see if she tasted as good as she smelled, because she smelled... amazing. She smelled like nature, the trees, and the wind, it seemed to be weaved into her soul. She also had an underlying sweetness that was all feminine.

And delicious.

Once I kissed her, I would move down her body. Touch every inch of her with my hands, and my lips. And if she let me slide inside of her, make us one, that moment would be the best moment of my long, miserable life.

She frowned and looked away. "You can tell me if I'm hurting you."

I stared. How did a man tell a woman that she was making him feel alive in a way he hadn't for years? "You're not hurting me."

She gave me a faint smile and began again, and then my worshipping, aroused thoughts turned on me. I was pining after Dawn Darkmore. A wealthy, beautiful vampire who was apparently now the leader of her clan, being challenged for her position. She needed to marry another powerful vampire.

If she was out of my reach as a poor human...she is certainly out of my reach as a freak warlock hybrid. Disbelief uncoiled within me, leaving my entire chest hurting in an entirely new way.

"So, you're a warlock then?" she asked in a voice that was too casual.

"A hybrid." I clenched my teeth. "Although after the experiments, I'm not sure if there's any human left in me."

She ran a hand over my stomach. "Well...you still feel human to me." Her words hung between us.

Did she mean that to sound so...sexy?

She finished dressing the bleeding wounds on my arms,

then slid from the couch. She parted my thighs, kneeling between them, moving her focus to the wounds on my stomach.

I caught myself before a groan could tear from my lips. I couldn't let her see how much she was affecting me. *She probably thinks I'm half-crazy. And I'm covered in bites from head to toe.* She'd probably be disgusted by my interest.

But even though I ordered myself to hide my attraction, my cock had a mind of its own. It rose eagerly, straining against the white towel I wore.

As she reached behind her for more Band-Aids, my gaze went to her chest. Her jumpsuit was dangerously low cut. From this angle, I could see straight down to the lacy white bra that held her breasts so lovingly.

My fingers twitched with the desire to reach out and touch her creamy flesh. Instead, I fisted my hands. *She's not mine to touch.*

When her elbow brushed my manhood, a groan tore from my lips.

My sensitive hearing picked up the way her heart suddenly started racing and the sound of her breathing as it became more rapid. I shook my head. My damn body wanted to imagine her response was a reciprocal attraction, but my mind told me that I was crazy.

"I'm so sorry they did this to you." Her hands brushed the skin of my chest, then lingered on my stomach. *Again.* It was pleasure and pain all in one. I had never ached so badly for another person.

"Is that where you went all those years ago when you vanished?"

She had noticed.

"I went for a hike. They found me and took me." I hadn't seen the light of day for three years after my capture. Three *long* years. And after that, I was watched. Always watched. A young man with confusing abilities and nowhere to go. *It wasn't hard to become their little soldier...at least their soldier with my moral limits...*

"I," she hesitated. "I was upset that you left without telling me. But after everything, I hoped maybe you found a woman, maybe even had a family."

I couldn't take my eyes off the way her lips pulled into a thin line. "I'm surprised you thought of me at all."

Her head jerked up. "Aiden..."

Yes?

She sighed. "Of course I did."

Was I imagining the pain in her eyes?

"I...we'd spoken only a few times." She continued after a moment. "But I thought..."

It was absolutely true. We'd spoken only a few times. But I was sure the bullies at the school left me alone because of something she did. I was sure the backpack and school supplies someone left for me each year in the office was from her. And the night my foster father disappeared, I didn't know how, but I felt sure she had something to do with it.

Afterward, a strange lawyer had been appointed to me. I successfully became emancipated, and someone had helped me to get a job as a maintenance worker in a crappy apartment building, but it paid my rent and left me money for food.

Even though it had seemed insane that a teenage girl could do all those things, my gut told me that she was involved.

Yet we had barely spoken, even though we saw each other every day at school. *Other than that night.*

"I know we were basically strangers," she said, dropping

a Band-Aid on the floor between us. "It was silly that I was so upset."

She leaned down to pick it up, and her cheek brushed my cock.

I inhaled sharply

She sat up and stared pointedly at my erection. Her tongue darted out to lick her lips.

Looking up at the ceiling, I sent a desperate thought out into the universe. *Damn my cruel imagination, stop it!*

Because in my mind, I saw her pulling back the folds of my towel to reveal the evidence of my desire. Her small hand curling around my girth as she pumped me slowly, and then faster and faster. And then her lips closing around me, taking my length into her hot mouth.

I shuddered, my eyes flying open as I felt my control slipping through my fingers. Grasping the side of my towel, I stood, scrambling away from her.

She stared, her eyes wide. "What's wrong?"

"Nothing." The word came out more harshly than I expected, so I added to it, trying to soften the blow, "Tomorrow we have a long day."

"But I wasn't finished!"

But I nearly was.

"It's good enough."

After a long minute, she nodded. "So tomorrow..."

"We find someone to help us find the communicator."

She walked across the room. "I'll change and then we can climb into bed."

Bed?

I looked at the one large bed dominating the back half of the cabin. Then I looked toward the celing and closed my eyes. *It looks like I won't be sleeping tonight.*

12

DAWN

WHEN I WAS sure that Aiden was asleep, I snuck away from the bed and grabbed my phone, before slipping outside. Once outside, I sat down on the porch steps and tried to shake off the feeling of Aiden so close behind me. We hadn't touched in bed, but the few inches of space between us almost made not touching even worse. It was like we were both trying our hardest not to, which made it even more uncomfortable. I felt like I was going crazy. I almost just pinned him down and had my way with him, rather than allow the building tension in my body to keep going until I shattered.

But then, I'd reminded myself that he was injured, had been through hell, and hadn't given a single indication that he was interested in me. Yeah, there had been something between us when I bandaged him up, at least I thought there had been, but it was just as likely that I had been imagining it, just because I wanted him to want me.

Even though it was late, almost two in the morning, I knew the person I was calling wouldn't mind. She always seemed to be awake when we were friends in Mist.

Hitting Sammi's phone number, I listened to it ringed with bated breath, until her groggy voice came over the line, "Hey, you okay?"

I nodded, then remembered she couldn't see me. "Yeah, I've just run into some trouble."

"Where are you? I can come get you," she doesn't sound tired any longer.

"No, it's not that bad. I just had some questions."

"For a Human Defender or for your friend Sammi?" she asked.

"Both. But unofficially," I said.

"Okay, shoot."

I don't really know where to start. "I found Aiden."

"Alive or dead?" she asked quietly.

"Alive."

Sammi was outside of my circle of friends in high school. She'd always just been kind of quiet, as if by being quiet no one would notice how naturally beautiful she was. I'd been partnered with her in science class and found her to be a strange human. She had the charisma of a supernatural, as well as, the beauty. But she completely lacked confidence. The only thing she seemed sure of was that one day she'd become a Human Defender.

I hated that I couldn't tell her that I was a vampire, but then she'd be obligated to tell her bosses, and every supernatural in Mist would be hunted down, punished, and removed from the city that was supposed to only have humans. As much as I wanted to tell my friend the truth, the risk was too great.

"So, are you going to tell me what happened to him?"

"Unofficially?" I stressed the word.

"Unofficially. This information goes with me to the grave."

I nodded to myself. "Okay. He was taken and experimented on by warlocks from another realm."

She was quiet. "Are you drunk?"

A laugh escaped my lips. "No. I swear it's true."

"Warlocks? Like, humans with magic?"

"Kind of," I admitted, feeling a bit foolish saying it aloud.

She released a slow breath. "Okay, I mean, I've been working as a Human Defender for a long time. And even though I've never heard of anything like that, this world is full of crazy bullshit, so I believe you. What do you need from me?"

"I don't know," I said, suddenly feeling lost. "The thing is...now, I'm expected to...take over my family's business. People don't think I'm up for the job and Aiden is willing to help me, but he needs to settle things with the warlocks first."

"That's a lot to handle," Sammi sounded like she wanted to reach through the phone and hug me. I only wished she could.

"It is," I brushed away a tear I hadn't realized had fallen. "I just don't know if I can do it all and keep Aiden safe and out of my heart."

Sammi's quiet for a long minute. "Listen, it isn't your job to keep everyone safe. Nor can you command your heart to feel a certain way. Believe me, my own heart's been broken by a guy, and I wish like hell I could forget all about him, but I can't. So, be easy on yourself. Don't put the weight of all of this on your shoulders, and give yourself time to see if there could be anything real between you and Aiden."

She was right. She was always right. "But I also feel torn

between my responsibility with my family and helping him with his task."

"If life was easy, it wouldn't be so damned hard," she said with a laugh. "Just try to focus on one thing at a time."

I released a slow breath. "Okay, thanks. And sorry to call so late."

"Nah, it's okay. I only just fell asleep after dealing with some massive sewer worm. It was eating people in the city. Literally, just popping out of sewer holes and eating them. I smell, literally like shit, and I've got to hunt some blood-suckers tomorrow."

"I don't envy you," I said, with a humorless laugh.

"I don't envy you either," she told me. "I know your parents left you and your brother their company, and that it must be nice to have money, but the one thing neither of us has now is a loving family, and that's worth more than anything."

"Just someone who always has our backs," I said.

"Who loves us unconditionally," she said, her voice no louder than a whisper.

Yeah, losing my family had been awful, but Sammi's father was one of the meanest humans I'd ever met. He treated her like she was a "slut" every time I was around him. He berated her and kept her on such a tight leash that every time I saw her, she looked dead inside. Like, she just wanted to disappear from the world. Leaving for the Human Defender school was probably the first time in her life that she didn't feel like a complete failure.

"Well, we always have each other," I told her. *Even though I'm hiding so much of myself from you.*

"Yeah, we do," but there was something hesitant in her voice too.

"Thanks for talking to me," I said.

"Always. Goodnight."

"Goodnight."

When the phone went dead, I shut it off and stood. But suddenly, a strange chill went down my spine. I looked into the darkness of the desert around me and had the unsettling feeling that I was being watched. It was probably just some animal, I tried to tell myself. The warlock shifters that had attacked us wouldn't have been able to scent us after traveling so far in my car. And no one else was after us. Right?

Still, the feeling lingered.

I decided to check the perimeter of the house. Going slowly, I watched everything around me, stretching out my vampiric senses. There were heartbeats around me. Too many to separate an animal from a dangerous enemy. I wished I could smell the way a shifter could, because maybe that would give me more information, but I wasn't about to wake Aiden over a feeling.

Still, I lingered in the shadows for a while until I was certain that it was just my nerves.

Climbing up the stairs, my phone suddenly buzzed. It was Layla, my Seer.

BE CAREFUL. *Danger is coming for you. Don't let down your guard.*

I HESITATED, then typed back.

THANK YOU.

. . .

GOING BACK INSIDE, I locked everything up tightly, then put another log on the fire. Before I climbed back into bed, I stared down at Aiden's face. Whatever danger was coming, I would protect him from it. No matter what it cost me. After so long of believing he'd just left town without saying good-bye, I would feel forever guilty that he had been through hell. If there had been one person in his life that cared enough about his disappearance to look into it, maybe he would have been okay.

I was that person. And even though I wasn't the one who hurt him, I sure as hell hadn't helped enough. I wouldn't make that mistake again. If he needed some communicator in Ghost Town before we could return to Mist, we would find it.

And then, all our enemies would pay.

13

*D*AWN

I SHIELDED my eyes with my hands as I looked up at the post office. It had a rugged look, very different from the charm of downtown Mist. It was a squat adobe structure with darkened windows and large cacti planted evenly around it.

This place is so different from Mist in every way.

Just the thought of my home sent a stabbing pain through my chest. I had to get back. My people needed me. But at the same time, Aiden's goal was no less important than my own. I could be delayed to protect innocent lives.

Although no matter how this ends, I'll be making certain the Shadow Keepers no longer have a home on Draven Cerberus's lands. Draven may think he'll usurp me soon, but until then, I am the overlord of all our lands, and I will get to the bottom of how the warlock shifters were able to conduct such awful things under our noses.

Especially if he had anything to do with it.

I glanced back at the post office, taking a deep breath.

Aiden needed to use this fairy to get the communications device. Then, we would leave Ghost Town, Arizona far behind and return to my lands.

Still, I felt tension crawling beneath my skin. There was so much to do, and time was of the essence. Besides that, I was tired. The bed we'd slept in last night had been much too small, and I'd been aware of his every movement. I could have sworn he didn't sleep well either.

My mother's voice floated through my mind. *"Smile, Dawn, never let them see what's below the surface. Your people want to see a flawless queen, not a person. You can never be a person to them. Familiarity breeds contempt."*

Looking down at my pale blue dress, expertly cut so the long, lightweight material flowed around my legs when I walked, I realized that I might look a tad out of place. The thought came and went in a flash. *Oscar de la Renta is always appropriate.*

It doesn't look like the kind of place a fairy would hang out, but who am I to judge? I patted the sides of my hair, feeling oddly nervous. I'd done a simple fishtail braid down my back, but without all my hair products, I worried it would come loose and look foolish.

Calm down, no one knows you're here. You don't have to be Dawn Darkmore. You can just be another girl. I dropped my hands, my anxiety lessening, even if it was still there.

"Ready?"

I turned to look at Aiden, who had just climbed out of the car. Luckily for him, he'd found an old plaid shirt and jeans at the cabin. Unfortunately for me, he looked so damned good, and the clothes were definitely a size too small. It'd been physically painful not to stare at his broad shoulders and tight ass. I'd gone from feeling like a figurehead to my people, to a hormonal teen the second I'd seen him.

Focus! I ordered myself, then forced my gaze up to his face.

Now, I fully expected him to be looking at the strange building in confusion too, but Aiden's gaze was slowly scanning the area around us, his eyes narrowed. The moment I realized something was off every muscle in my body tensed, and my thoughts of how amazing he looked faded away.

"What is it?"

After a long second, he answered, "Nothing."

But it sure as hell didn't seem like nothing, as he continued staring around us as if waiting for an attack at any moment. Yet, he didn't tell me a thing. And being left in the dark ticked me off. We were in this together, right? So I had a right to know if something was going on.

"You sure?"

"Yeah," he said, but he didn't sound the least bit convincing.

I raised a brow and planted a hand on my hip, his gaze snapped to me, but his blank expression told me he didn't have a clue why I seemed upset. Tapping the toes of my beautiful leather thigh-high boots, I let out a slow breath when his blank expression turned to a confused one..

He isn't your brother. He isn't going to be able to read your every thought before you can voice it.

Yet, I'd never really been good at explaining how I felt.

Luckily for me, he finally started talking. "I just," he shrugged as he said, "feel like we're being watched."

Every good feeling quickly vanished. *Watched?* I squinted my eyes in the bright morning sun and scanned the quiet street to one side and the desert to the other. Was there really something out there?

"I felt that way last night."

"When?" his entire body tensed.

I avoided his gaze. "When I went outside to make a call."

"A call?" He sounded upset. "If you were going to go outside, you should have told me."

I lifted a brow, meeting his gaze. "I can take care of myself."

His frown deepened. "Who did you need to call so late? And why did you need to take the call outside?"

I stiffened, feeling defensive. "None of your business."

He looked like I'd slapped him, but before I could soften my words, he said, "You're right. It isn't any of my business who you're connected to. This is a business relationship. You're helping me, so I'll help you, and that's all."

"I didn't mean it--"

"It's fine," he said, then glanced around us again. "But we need to be careful."

His dismissal of me hurt, but I decided to follow his lead with changing the conversation away from what our relationship was or wasn't. "Do you think it's *them*?"

Are those warlocks still hunting Aiden? It makes sense they wouldn't have given up on their search to find the communications device.

"I don't know. But let's head inside. And be careful."

As we walked to the door, his long strides meant I fell behind. My gaze instantly went to his incredible ass. *Again.*

Damn it.

I hated how good he looked. The jeans hugged his hard ass and clung to the bulge in his pants. Even the shirt looked like it was about to explode off him like the Incredible Hulk. It stretched tightly at the shoulders, and I got to see peeks of his hard stomach and chest where the buttons were pulled too tightly.

"Coming?" he asked, holding open the door and looking utterly confused.

I shook myself, ducking my head as I hurried toward him, so he couldn't see me blushing. *What's wrong with me? Yes, he looks good, but I need to show more control than this!*

But I didn't have time to consider it further because I was suddenly overwhelmed by a room that was smaller than my great-aunt's cabin and cluttered with cheesy Western decor. Shelves by the door had dead scorpions preserved in glittery, plastic half domes, postcards with half-naked cowboys, and a variety of other odds and ends.

I reached out and touched one of the scorpions with my fingertip and smiled. Ghost Town was certainly an interesting place, but it was growing on me more and more each day. *It was fun visiting as a kid, but seeing it through adult eyes is certainly different.*

When I reached for a little statue of a lizard, it suddenly moved.

A shriek exploded from my lips, and I swore the lizard stared at me for a long second before taking off.

"It was just a lizard," Aiden said.

I released a huff of breath. "I know. The thing just scared me."

A man suddenly cleared his throat.

I whirled to see that a man, well, a dwarf, had climbed onto a stool behind the counter. One of his brows was raised in question at us.

Aiden crossed the small space and put his hands on the counter, leaning forward ever so slightly. "I'm looking for a fairy named Sabrina."

The dwarf's lips puckered. He may have been far shorter than Aiden, yet he had the attitude of a giant as he spoke. "And who's asking about her?"

Aiden's eyes narrowed.

I sighed, and strode toward them, placing a hand on his shoulder. "I'm Lucilla's great-great-niece, or something like that. We're looking for an item that we lost, and Aunt Lucilla indicated that Sabrina might be just the one to help with the job." Then, I flashed him a smile.

His anger instantly melted away, and he ran his hands through his strawberry blond hair. "Well, why didn't he just say that? You must be Dawn."

"Why—yes, how did you know?"

He grinned and leaned forward, winking as his gaze ran over me. "She told us all about you. She said not to be mistaken about your vampire looks, that you were a fae through and through."

Oh boy, who else has my aunt told that I'm here—and will that complicate things further?

"Is Sabrina here, or not?" Aiden asked, his words clipped.

The dwarf looked from him to me. "How come all the beautiful girls like the brooding, dangerous guys? You know dwarves are well-known for their charm, wit, good manners, and—"

"Ability to waste the time of those around them," Aiden interrupted, folding his arms over his chest.

The dwarf's eyes flashed with anger.

Great. This little manly argument isn't getting us anywhere.

I patted his shoulder again. "What my big, grumpy friend here means is that we're pressed for time. Is she here?"

After a moment, the dwarf huffed and turned behind him, shouting, "Sabrina! You got people here for you!"

A second later, a younger woman, about a head shorter than me, walked out of the door to the back. She had the delicate features of a fairy, with curly blond hair and deep brown eyes. The golden, glittery dress she wore added to the illusion, delicate spaghetti straps and an outward flare at the bottom reminded me of a modern version of a fairy tale. Her skin glittered slightly, whether it was due to a glamour or actual glitter, I wasn't sure.

"Tell those twins they need to find another game to play because I'm done with their—?" Her gaze went to Aiden and her eyes widened. Her lips formed into an O, and she simply came to a stop. "Wow!"

The dwarf rolled his eyes. "They need you."

Sabrina strolled right up to Aiden and leaned forward, only the counter between them. "You wanted me?" Her voice was husky, and frankly, desperate.

Seriously? Does this fairy really think Aiden would be interested in someone who can't be older than nineteen? Although, I have no idea what Aiden's type is...

"*We* wanted your help," I said, straightening my shoulders.

The fairy didn't look at me, but her smile for Aiden grew wider. "What can I do for you?"

Aiden didn't seem to notice that the girl was almost drooling on him. "I'm looking for a lost item."

"I'll help you with anything you need. Anything at all."

He nodded. "Thank you. Can you help us now?"

She put her hands on the counter and climbed over, practically knocking me over in her haste. "I'd go anywhere with you."

Aiden looked to the dwarf. "Do you have a map of the area?"

The other man looked more than a little annoyed. "There's a pile of free ones right over there, pretty boy."

Aiden ignored both him and the fairy, crossed the room,

picked up a map and brought it back. He spread it out on the counter, then peered down at it. I came closer and looked at it too. This area was one big desert. How were we supposed to find something so small in all of this?

"What are we looking for?" Sabrina whispered, leaning down closer to him, her nipples brushing his arm.

I glared at her. "Like we said, something we lost."

After a minute, Aiden grabbed a pen from the counter and circled a spot on the map. "Something here."

She leaned in closer to him. "I'll need more to go on than that."

He frowned. "It's a metal...device. It looks like this." He drew a picture of something on the top of the map that looked like a metal walkie-talkie. "Is this enough for you to work with?"

She looked from the picture to the spot circled on the map. "It should be."

"Great," he said. "Let's go."

We walked back to my Bentley.

Sabrina grinned. "I can sit in the back with you."

I've had about enough of you. "He'll sit in the front."

The fairy pouted, but got into the back, slamming the door behind her.

When I got into the car, I gunned the engine. "Just tell me where to go."

Aiden stared at the map. "To the right. It's in the middle of nowhere, probably a half hour from here."

Sabrina leaned forward and put one of her elbows on the backs of each of the bucket seats. "Good, that'll give us time to get to know each other better."

"Sit back and hook your seat belt," I ordered. "I don't want your glitter all over my white leather seats."

I looked over my shoulder to make sure the girl had

followed directions, then glanced sideways at Aiden before looking ahead.

For the first time, his lips had turned upward into a slight grin.

I sighed. Was he really enjoying how annoying I found the woman? Or was he enjoying all the attention she was giving him? I might have known the boy he once was, but I had no idea who he had grown into. Maybe he was hooking up with young women every damn day.

Can this day get any worse?

He crossed his arms over his chest, and I could feel his eyes on me. "I can't actually remember seeing you frustrated when we were younger."

"That's because I usually killed people who irritated me this badly." The second the words left my mouth, I felt sick. "I mean, I didn't hang out with people who bothered me this much."

To my surprise, he reached out and squeezed my knee. "I knew what you meant."

I felt my tension ease at his touch. *First Lucilla hugs me, and then this.* It was ridiculous how much it meant to me to have someone in my life that wasn't afraid of me.

He pulled his hand away, but the spot he touched stayed warm.

Maybe today won't be so bad after all.

14

AIDEN

As WE TRAVELED, I became more and more agitated. All day I'd sensed that we were being watched, but I could see nothing to justify my concerns. There wasn't even the slightest scent of the warlock pack.

I drummed my fingers on my knee wishing I could shift. My primal urge to run as hard as my body would allow was like an itch I couldn't scratch. My injuries were healing at a rapid pace, my broken arm only sore rather than excruciating. And I no longer bled, but every wound still felt too tight. Sitting in a car was the last place I should be, both for the good of my body and my anxious thoughts.

After all these years of experimentation, and months of running from them, I'm being paranoid.

Or perhaps I'm just on edge...being so close to Dawn and knowing she's not mine. I froze, thinking of the private call she'd made, apparently after I'd fallen asleep. As hard as I tried, I couldn't think of anyone besides a lover she would have contacted, and the idea of her with someone else bothered me more than I cared to admit, even if just to myself.

Dawn had everything. I had nothing. Just like when we were kids. I was a man who couldn't offer her anything that she deserved, beyond being her champion in the fight to keep her title. So, I wouldn't delude myself into thinking that we could be more than that. No matter how much I hated thinking about a future that didn't include her.

Not that I'm likely to survive all of this. I pushed the thought aside. *No, my mood has nothing to do with Dawn and everything to do with the damn warlocks.*

Logically, I doubted that Dawn had scared the warlocks off so easily, even with her touch of death power. Without the communications device the shifters would never make it home, and to them, being on Earth was a never-ending prison sentence.

I smirked. The pack of warlocks had been prisoners of the Magic Police, a police force that worked across all realms and stopped criminals from hurting people in less advanced realms. They'd managed to break free of prison, steal a vessel, and take off thinking they could hide out in a primitive realm until their big bad boss could pick them up.

At least that's what I gathered from what I overhead.

I thought I'd broken the only communications device they had. But when I'd overheard that they were trying to retrieve the same type of device from another crashed ship, I'd realized I couldn't just save myself and turn my back on the rest of humanity. I was one of the few who knew what these criminals could do. Personally.

No, as much as I want to be finished with those damn warlocks, I need to do this first.

"Uh," the fairy said, her more serious voice instantly

drawing my attention. "It's that way." She pointed to a random direction off the road.

My heart pounded and my palms grew sweaty. *This is it. We're getting closer.*

Dawn slowed the car and started to turn.

My gaze swung to her before I could stop it. I remembered when the only thing I thought I knew of vampires was that they were sensitive to sunlight and that they were bloodsucking monsters. Yet, here she sat, the sunlight streaming over her, as calm and beautiful as ever.

When she'd joined me outside that morning, I'd nearly forgotten to breathe. The dress she wore clung to every curve of her incredible body, dipping low in the front. I'd had the overwhelming desire to slide my hands into the front of her dress and cup her full breasts, to roll her nipples until she groaned.

And the skirt of her dress? It was slit so damn high up the side that I could see the lace of her panties. Actually, all I could see was lace. *Maybe it's a G-string.*

I shifted uncomfortably. *If I laid her back on a bed, it would take nothing at all to bury myself inside her.*

Worse, I knew from the way her nipples hardened when the air-conditioning hit them that she wasn't wearing a bra. And the top of the dress had a wide neck. Very wide. *Wide enough to slip down without taking it off.* Pulling the map down, I pressed it over my obvious erection. *How can I possibly concentrate on my mission with her around driving me crazy?*

That's why I decided not to look at her, which I keep failing to actually do!

The car suddenly started to shake as we left the small patch of smooth dirt and continued on into the vast desert. But I was more than grateful for the distraction.

"Ma'am, you don't want to do that—"

Do what?

"Don't call me 'ma'am'," Dawn interrupted. "We're almost the same age."

"You mean you're almost the same age as my mom," Sabrina huffed.

Dawn's hands tightened on the steering wheel. "No, you just act half our age. You'd better watch it or—"

I interrupted, "Why didn't you want us to turn off the road? You said to go this way."

If there was actual danger, and not just my paranoia, I'd never risk putting two innocent people in danger. My hands closed into fists. I needed to get this device, and I needed their help, but I wouldn't risk their lives to do it. *What had the fairy sensed that I hadn't?*

Sabrina huffed. "Because, am I the only one who realizes we're in a Bentley? I mean, these things have got to be what, a hundred thousand dollars?"

Oh. That.

Dawn smirked. "It costs more with the options, but, no matter."

"You *sure*?" the fairy emphasized. "Because we could just get out and walk..."

She shrugged. "It's just a car."

Things had never mattered to Dawn as much as to other people. Anytime someone in their classes needed something, whether it was money for lunch or something bigger, we quickly received it. She was never obvious about it, but I always *knew* she was responsible. And now, the more time I spent with Dawn, the more I realized she hadn't changed a bit in all these years.

And I liked that. *Too much. But my feelings mean nothing,*

because rich and powerful vampires simply don't end up with someone damaged like me.

Once I'm finished being her champion, she'll probably send me on my way, happy to be safe with her lover.

"If you don't care what you drive, then why have a flashy car like this?" the fairy asked, cocking her head to one side in a haughty fashion.

Dawn flashed her a smile that was all teeth and two very sharp-looking canines. "Because I can."

For the first time in longer than I could remember, I smiled. *Typical Dawn.* She was always so damn good at putting on a show.

"Do you even need a car? Can't you just...you know, change into a cute, fuzzy bat and fly around?" Sabrina asked, a challenge in her words.

A bat? Everyone knew vampires couldn't turn into bats. It was a mean stereotype.

Dawn smirked. "Why don't you just flap your wings and take us there?"

Sabrina huffed in response.

It might have been awkward except suddenly the fairy reached across us to point in one direction. Over the next few minutes, Sabrina was constantly pointing in one direction or another, putting Dawn's vampire reflexes to the test. Dawn swerved around trees, shrubs, cacti, and boulders with ease.

At first, all I could think about was how the bouncing vehicle brought to life my still-healing injuries. My stomach felt hollow as I clenched my teeth down on hiss after hiss of pain. I needed to focus on something else. Anything else.

And then I glanced at Dawn, and my pain faded away.

Her full breasts bounced enticingly the entire way. I told myself I wouldn't stare. But I did. *Man, wolf or warlock, it doesn't matter, I'm still a man*. And if the fairy girl hadn't been in the back, I wasn't sure I could have controlled myself. Her breasts were begging to be fondled, her nipples pleading to be teased. My hands twitched with the need to touch her.

"Are we getting closer?" Dawn reached across me and placed a hand on my thigh. "Do you want to double-check the map?"

Are you kidding me? I was breathing hard, unable to answer. *Are you aware that your hand is inches from my straining manhood? Because if it goes any closer, I'm going to forget about the fairy in the back.*

"He doesn't need to check the map," the fairy answered, sounding annoyed. "We're almost there."

I already knew there was no point in looking at the map. The communications device was close, but the location was so vague that the map couldn't help any further. That's why we needed the fairy in the first place.

But then I saw something familiar...

"There!" I shouted, pointing.

Dawn slammed on her brakes.

To one side, a saguaro cactus that looked like a man giving a thumbs-up stood proud and tall. "I remember that cactus from their map."

The fairy nodded. "I sense we're close. It wouldn't hurt to get out here."

I nodded. I guess this was it. Hopefully, soon, I'd find the device, contact the asshole's police force, and get them out of here. Humans would be safe. Well, safer. And I could move on with my life.

15

AIDEN

DAWN CUT THE ENGINE, and we all piled out into the hot summer morning. I tried to keep myself calm, but I kept thinking back to what I'd seen in that damned lab. I kept imagining all the humans still being tortured there. In my mind, the screams of those people in cages rolled through me until every hair on my body stood on end.

I remembered what those needles felt like when they pierced my skin. I remembered being eighteen, barely a man, and begging them until I was hoarse to let me go.

Calm down. Focus. Focus on your task.

If I couldn't communicate with the right people, not only would those people be screwed, but all of humanity would be in danger. The warlocks would continue stealing humans off of the streets, experiment on them, and leave their bodies everywhere. And every life that would be lost would be on me. Because I was the only one who could stop this.

"You okay?" Dawn asked.

And I realized those startling hazel eyes were locked on me. "Fine."

The fairy took the map, looked at the drawing of the device again, and closed her eyes. For a long time, we stood without moving. The air was hot and dry. The bright sunlight reflected off the desert floor, glimmering like a mirage in the distance.

"This way," she said.

Then, she looked back at me. "It would help if you could take my arm. It's hard to focus on where my feet are when I'm trying to *feel* for the lost item."

I scrambled over and took her arm.

Dawn followed behind us at a slower pace. Her expression guarded.

We walked for twenty long minutes before Sabrina suddenly stopped.

"There's something here...but it doesn't feel right."

I scanned the desert. It was just an endless landscape of dirt, and the squat, brown and pale green plants that stubbornly grew.

"It looks the same," I said, my frustration growing.

Sabrina shook her head. "There's something." She raised her hand and then pointed straight in front of us. "There, but it's hidden."

"Under the dirt?" *We really should have brought shovels.*

"No, it's concealed by...magic, like nothing I've felt before. Luckily, I've got something perfect for this situation."

Reaching into the folds of her shimmery dress, she pulled out a bottle filled with dust the color of blood. "This should do it."

She popped off the top. "My friend, a fairy with an interest in experimenting, has been making this stuff for me for years."

"Since you were in diapers?" Dawn said, the corner of her mouth twitching.

"I'll have you know I'm twenty-six," Sabrina responded, jerking her chin up.

Dawn's eyes widened. "There's no chance we're almost the same age!"

Sabrina smiled and patted my arm. "Some women just hide their age better."

I stared at them, utterly confused. *Why are we wasting time talking about this nonsense?* "Is the item I'm looking for here?"

Sabrina's smile grew as she looked back at the tube of powder in her hands. "Just watch this."

With practiced movements, she sprinkled a little in her hand. Then, locking eyes with me, she spoke a few soft words that I couldn't quite catch. Her lips curled, and then she blew.

The red grains lifted off her hand slowly, rising and spinning as if they were smoke curling up from a fire. With each second that passed, they seemed to multiply, spinning faster and faster. Wind began to tug at me. My clothes flapped, and the swirling red formed into a small tornado.

What the hell is this? The magic likely wasn't dangerous, but I wasn't taking any chances. I went to Dawn, pulling her to my side. To my relief, she wrapped her arms around my neck in return. And suddenly, her smaller body was pressed against mine.

I forgot about the tornado. Forgot about everything except the feel of her in my arms. The wind tore around us and I closed my eyes, pressing my face against her hair, shielding her face in the crook of my arm and chest. Nothing was more important than holding her against me and the incredible feeling of knowing that she was seeking comfort from me.

When the wind began to die down, I looked up from where I'd pressed my face into her sweet-smelling hair. I coughed, the dust in the air heavy. The air too clouded to see. But then, the dust dropped like a curtain, and the air was instantly clear once more.

I'll never get used to magic.

Her lips brushed my throat, and her grip loosened as her hands slid down my chest. I inhaled sharply, unsure if her touch was intentional. Unsure if she knew the havoc she was playing on my body.

My arousal grew. My hands tightened on her hips. "Dawn?"

Does she feel something between us too? Or am I crazy?

"Wow!" Sabrina cried.

My head snapped up, the moment broken as I remembered where I was and what we were after. There, not twenty feet in front of us, was something that looked like a mix between a boat and a spaceship. It was the size of a car, with a huge white sail, and a sleek, white bottom. Everything about it screamed that it wasn't from our realm, from the sleekness of the metal to the strange glint from the sails. My gaze ran from one perfectly intact side to the front that was slightly crumpled in.

This must be where the communications device is hidden.

Dawn slipped from my grip and hesitantly moved forward, running her hands over the shining surface. "It's... amazing. So smooth. And still cool, as if the sun wasn't shining on it."

That prickling on the back of my neck started again. I inhaled slowly. I scented dust, a few small animals, but no warlock shifters. *Then why do I feel so restless?*

"Let's just get it and get out," I said curtly.

Both women looked up at me sharply, but after a second, Dawn nodded. "Probably a good idea."

I ran my hand along the outside of the ship, looking for the entrance. There had to be a button, something to open it. But I felt nothing.

The fairy laid her hand on mine.

I stiffened, but she tugged my hand over to one spot.

"Right here."

A blue ring of light formed where my hand touched, and slowly a door opened on the side of the ship. Inside, there was a small compartment, big enough for one large person, and a dashboard.

For one brief moment, I stared in amazement. This was an actual craft that someone had flown between realms! What happened to the warlock who had flown it? And was this warlock the same awful species who had tortured me, or something entirely different?

"Whoa," the fairy breathed, bringing me back to reality.

Right. The communications device.

Focusing, I let my gaze slide over every inch of the ship. *Did I come all this way for nothing?* Panic started to set in. And then I saw it, tucked against the seat. Holding my breath, I reached in and pulled it free. As my arm slid past the dashboard, a dozen tiny lights flashed on. *It works. After all this time?*

Damn warlock technology.

I looked away from the strange ship to the thing I'd risked my life to find. The device fit perfectly in my hand, a smooth orb with a speaker, a small screen, a dial, and a couple of buttons. *Using this, I'll finally be able to stop anyone else from being tortured the way I was. I'll finally be able to sleep at night.*

But first, I need to get us out of here. To somewhere safe.

"Got it, time to go."

As I turned, I caught it, the slightly reptilian scent of the warlock shifters. My stomach turned and a cold sweat washed over my body. "Damn. They're here…"

"Who?" the fairy asked, frowning.

But Dawn answered before I could. "Shifters. Dangerous ones."

The color drained from the fairy's face. "What do they want?"

I clenched the device harder in my hand. "This. And they probably want us dead, as well." But maybe between the three of us, we can do *something.* "Sabrina, what kind of magic do you have? Can you help us?"

The fairy backed away from us, shaking her head. "Sorry, I'm out. This…this wasn't what I signed on for."

Dawn looked down her nose at the fairy angrily. "You're not going anywhere by yourself. We're in the middle of the desert. Where do you think you're going to go? We all need to make it back to the car."

The scent of the warlocks was everywhere. *Too close.* "We won't make it there in time," I said.

Sabrina put the bottle with the red dust back in the pocket of her dress and then pulled out another one with blue dust. Her eyes were wide as she glanced at the desert around her.

A howl vibrated through the air.

I stiffened and moved closer to Dawn, widening my stance and preparing for battle.

"Sorry, guys," Sabrina whispered.

I glanced back at her and witnessed her tossing the blue dust over her head. Instantly, she vanished.

There goes any chance we had. Now what?

"Where the hell did she go?" Dawn's hands curled into fists. "And why didn't she take us with her?"

I shook my head. It didn't matter. What mattered was protecting Dawn. If we started running, out in the open like this, we couldn't possibly survive against the warlock shifters. But what choice did we have?

My gaze landed on the ship, and a desperate plan started to form. "We need to get in the ship."

"The broken ship?" she asked in complete disbelief. Her voice rose two octaves. "With enough room for only one person?"

I didn't answer her. Instead, I lifted her into my arms, even though the half-healed wounds on my torso and arms cried out in protest, and climbed into the ship with her across my lap. The fit was tight. But when the door slowly slid shut, I sent a prayer that this might just be our escape. Around us, the metal shimmered, then becem see-through, like glass. We could see everywhere around us, except directly under us.

Desperate, I started pushing buttons.

A crackled voice spoke in a language I didn't under-stand. "*Gfthguy*?"

To his shock, Dawn mimicked the voice back. "*Gfhgui.*" Or a word close to the one spoken.

"What does that mean?" I asked.

"I don't know, I don't speak warlock," she replied tensely.

Instantly, the ship responded. It started to shake as the lights on the dashboard flickered and changed different colors.

And that's when a face appeared outside, leaning on the side of the ship. Long dark hair framed a pale face that was twisted in rage. *Aghader.*

"Can he see us?" Dawn asked, cringing back into my chest.

"Who cares? As long as he can't get in here we'll be okay."

"But they're warlocks! They probably know exactly how to get in!" Her voice was rising again.

I looked out at them cautiously. "I don't think so. If they knew how to open it, they would have done it by now."

The warlock shifter's white cloudy eye, surrounded by scars, was glowing. Howls rose around the ship, and then I felt the warlocks slamming against the sides, pitching the vessel slightly one way and then another. Aghader curled his hands into fists and then slammed them down on the glass-like material.

Please let this damn warlock technology hold out against them!

I started hitting buttons again, desperate. If I couldn't get the ship to work, I'd just trapped myself and Dawn. I'd destroyed any chance that we might escape.

The strange warlock voice spoke again. "*Jtffurie?*"

"*Jtfury,*" Dawn spoke back, her voice edged with panic.

The ship's shaking grew more and more intense, and then, the door began to slide open. *No! He found the button!* I frantically hit the spot that closed the door, but it didn't respond.

This can't be happening!

Aghader's long arm reached into the opening, his hand trying to grip the front of Dawn's dress.

She reached out, her movements quick and sure, and snapped his wrist.

Aghader screamed, a bloodcurdling sound. His hand lay limply just above them, a bone sticking out of one side as blood gushed down over them.

The ship started to lift off the ground, and Aghader pulled his hand free just in time.

I hit the button over and over again to close the door to our side, when at last the ship responded. The door continued closing as we started to rise into the air. Our vessel slowly pitched forward, until we were flung against the dashboard and the roof. Peering down, we took in the ground forty feet below us.

A dozen angry wolves prowled, paced, leaped toward us, with Aghader standing in the center, his eyes filled with rage. I sensed in them their need for blood. Their need to destroy their enemy.

But they can't reach us.

"Thank God!" Dawn exclaimed. "I thought we were—"

Then, the ship started to sink. The lights on the dashboard dulled. And we moved downward, every inch closer to certain death.

"What's happening?" she asked, her words laced with panic.

I didn't answer. Instead, I started to slam the buttons.

The warlock voice began again, softer and more garbled.

Dawn repeated back to it, but nothing happened.

"Damn it," I shouted. "I think that's warlock for 'you're screwed.'"

A warlock leaped in front of us, only missing our ship by a few feet.

We're screwed.

16

DAWN

MY MIND RACED as I tried to repeat back every word the ship spoke, but nothing happened. I looked at our enemy drawing closer as we continued to fall slowly toward the ground. My vampiric teeth elongated. If they thought they could kill us, that they could hurt Aiden again, they had no idea who they faced. I might have lost my touch of death, but they would quickly learn that I was quite adept at killing without it.

Every muscle in my body tensed as a warlock shifter jumped on the front of our ship, followed by three others. The wolves' nails scraped at the glass-like material on the ship's hood, but they failed to find purchase, and tumbled back to the ground.

I shifted in Aiden's lap, wishing I had my legs beneath me, that I could easily leap from the vessel and take them by surprise if needed. *The odds aren't in our favor, but I always gamble on living.*

More wolves hit the front of the ship when a deafening roar filled the air. The wolves turned and fell from the front of the ship. I looked to the side, and a chill ran over my skin.

A dragon flew straight toward us. It had black scales and was massive in size, smoke billowed from its nostrils, and I could also sense its anger. What was worse, I knew the dragon wanted to be seen, because it didn't conceal itself with magic. *What kind of dragon doesn't care if it's seen?* Probably one that wanted us scared before it killed us.

"Uh...dragon," I said, hitting Aiden in the chest, and trying to keep my voice from shaking.

"I saw it," he muttered, still fooling with the controls, making the sail above us shift one way and then the other, but neither direction lifted us higher.

I glanced at it again. The dragon was still barreling toward us. Straight toward us, and we had no idea how to get out of its way.

"Aren't you worried?" I asked, trying not to sound as scared as I felt.

"Yes. But there's not a hell of a lot I can do if this ship doesn't move." He punched a button and the lights outside the craft turned on.

"Great. Maybe it's afraid of light."

As I spied the smoke still pouring from its nostrils, I realized this dragon was much more dangerous than the shifters. Those teeth could probably chomp right through the spaceship if he chose to.

"Who do you think it's coming for?" I asked worriedly.

"At best? The warlocks. And that probably includes me." His serious gaze pierced mine. "At worst? It's just hungry. So that's all of us."

A second later, its shadow covered us. Enormous talons

closed around our ship, and suddenly, we were pulled into the sky.

"Oh shit. I guess it just wants us." Aiden said, and somehow that thought didn't make me feel any better.

I pressed myself against the window to watch the wolves. Below us, the warlock shifters gave chase on land for several seconds. And then, before my eyes, transformed into scaled birds the size of large dogs.

Hell. They're really warlocks. Really creatures that can take on any shape. There was no denying it now, even if I didn't believe Aiden, I'd never seen anything like them before.

The creatures looked like poor imitations of a dragon. Instead of looking fantastical and beautiful, like the one holding us, the warlocks had become hideous, gray with yellow eyes and grotesquely shaped spiked bodies. They flapped their wings, wings that looked slick. Wet.

A dozen of the horrific creations lifted off the ground and gave chase.

I looked between the dragon and us. "What's the plan here?"

Aiden inhaled slowly, and I turned to look at him. Realization suddenly dawned on his face. "I know that dragon! It's the police officer. It's Paul. When we met him, he smelled like a bigger predator, but I couldn't tell what he was. I've never met a dragon shifter before." He sounded awed.

I released the breath I didn't know I was holding. "So, at least we know he's on our side. But what about them?"

He turned and looked at the warlock shifters, who, strangely enough, were rapidly gaining on us. His face paled. "This isn't good. I've never seen them shift into anything else before. I think keeping the wolf shifter facade was important to them. The fact that they don't care now means they're so desperate they don't care who finds out."

"So what can we do to help Paul?"

He shook his head. "Nothing while we're in the air."

A morbid sense of curiosity overtook me. "You absolutely can't change into...something else?"

"Not that I know of." His expression became guarded. "Only a wolf."

"That's...too bad. It could have been an advantage right now."

The warlock shifters drew closer. *Does Paul see them?*

"Paul!" I shouted, pointing behind us at our enemies.

The dragon cocked its head and one enormous, yellow-slitted eye peered in at me, and then back at the pack of frightening mutant dragons. He roared again, so loudly it shook our ship.

Paul suddenly halted in midair, turning and flapping his great wings so we hovered in place. And then, fire blasted from his mouth.

Two of the warlocks caught fire, and their blazing bodies went tumbling to the earth far below.

That works.

A change seemed to ripple through the warlocks. They halted in midair as well, eyeing the dragon and glancing at each other.

They know he's on our side now.

I watched with bated breath as, very slowly, the warlocks turned around and went the opposite direction. "Thank God!"

Aiden's arms wrapped around me more tightly. "I don't like owing people favors, but this is one time I'm grateful for it. Paul got here just in the nick of time."

"And you got your communications device." I let my head fall back onto his chest, the anxiety melting from me.

We might currently be in a broken ship carried by a dragon, but at least for one moment, we were safe.

His hand touched my hair, hesitantly, and my heart began to race again. And then, he slowly stroked my hair, finishing with his fingertips caressing my back.

I listened to the pounding of his heart, wondering if it was due to what we had been through, or if it was because we were currently in a small space, with me across his lap. I hoped the latter.

My fingers began to play with the buttons on his shirt, my fingertips grazing the bare flesh between them.

"Dawn, I..."

I stilled. "Yes?"

"I'm sorry I got you involved in all of this." His head bowed and his shoulders hunched slightly.

"That's okay," I said the words, but felt strangely disappointed. "Life for any magical creature is dangerous. Besides, when we get to Mist, I'll be dragging you into my chaos."

He chuckled, the sound raspy. "I guess we'll be even then."

Shifting in his lap, I was surprised when I felt his arousal. *So I do affect him!*

I lifted my head from his chest, and his hand dropped from my hair. I couldn't tear my gaze away from his, even as a wave of uncertainty threatened to sweep me under. It still felt unbelievable that my champion was Aiden. That he was back in my life after all this time.

If my powers were gone forever, and if both he and my people would be safe, I think I could love him. Maybe I've always loved him.

But that's a lot of ifs. And a lot of maybe's.

And what if my powers were still there, lingering beneath the surface, waiting to claim yet another person I loved?

My stomach twisted. Could I risk it?

No. Never.

It was a terrible irony. I couldn't save my people as a powerless woman, but I couldn't love Aiden either because my powers might still be there, lurking in the depths of my magic. It felt like a cruel slap from the hand of fate. A lump formed in my throat, and I looked away from him.

I wanted to be angry. Scream. Break something. But instead, I was desperately trying not to cry. This man deserved someone who would protect him. Someone who could make up for every awful thing he'd experienced in his life.

There was one side of me that imagined him running Darkmore by my side. He would make a damn good leader. He was strong. Good. Protective of those who were weaker than him. What he'd gone through to get the communicator proved that.

And at Darkmore, he would be safe. Protected by guards. Protected by high walls. Protected by his vampire wife who would destroy anyone who dared to harm him.

Yet, you cannot promise that he'll be safe from you.

And so, I couldn't take him for my own. I couldn't give him all the things I wished, even if I wanted to.

"Dawn?" He touched my cheek, but I refused to look at him. "It's okay. I understand."

His words were so gentle. I buried my face in his neck and wrapped one hand around his nape to tangle my fingers in his short hair. This man, half-human, half-warlock, whatever, he smelled so good, so sweet. Masculine. An intoxicating scent mixed with the rich fragrance of the earth. *And also?* I inhaled again. Something I'd never smelled before. Something...warlock.

A shudder racked my body, and I felt my inner muscles squeeze. His scent aroused me. Something that had never happened before in my life.

I had fed many times on willing, living humans, but never before had I fed because I knew the intoxicating taste of someone would bring me over the edge. Never had I fed in a moment of sexual pleasure. *And feeding to eat and feeding to taste a lover are two entirely different things.*

Oh, how he tempted me! But if I sank my teeth into the soft flesh of his throat, every ounce of willpower within me would evaporate, and I would take him here and now.

This is not the time, or the place. And you know you'll have to let him go.

Clamping down on a moan, I pulled back from him and wrapped my arms around myself. Took deep breaths. Told myself not to touch him again.

Above us, the dragon's grip changed, causing the ship to jerk. And then, the dragon released us. For one minute, we were falling. A scream tore from my lips.

The ship hit the ground a second later.

I panted, struggling to right myself. "Where are we?"

"I don't know." Aiden hit the glass-like material of the ship, and a blue ring radiated from the spot he touched, as the door of the ship slowly drew back. "But it's definitely time to get out."

I climbed free the second there was enough room for me to squeeze out. Falling onto the dirt of the desert floor, I climbed to my feet, dusting off my dress. When I straightened, I looked behind the ship. We were back at the cabin.

"We made it!" I said with a laugh.

Aiden launched himself out of the ship, hitting the dirt behind me, and then pulled me into a hug. "I was sure we were—"

"I know." I laughed again and drew back from him, our eyes meeting.

For a minute, the heat of his touch on my hips seemed to sear my flesh, uncurling heat throughout my entire body. *Whoa!*

Taking a step back from him, I swallowed and looked away. "And we got the device."

His gaze turned upward, and he spoke after a long second. "I can't believe all of this could be over with soon. Years of pain, experiments, and suffering. I can make sure it doesn't happen to anyone else."

"At least one problem will be over," I said with a humorless laugh. "We still have Darkmore to deal with."

"Don't worry, I didn't forget."

Paul came out from behind the house a minute later. His cowboy hat askew, his shirt buttoned incorrectly. "I thought you both promised me no more trouble."

Aiden looked down at his shoes. "Sorry, sir."

The police officer straightened his shoulders and scanned over Aiden. "It looks like you have some explaining to do."

Behind him, the door of the cabin opened. Out came Lucilla and Sabrina. The fairy's cheeks were bright pink.

I straightened my spine and walked toward them. "We're really sorry. We just—"

Lucilla threw her arms around me, pulling me close. "I'm so glad you're back and you're safe."

I was shocked when my eyes prickled with tears. What

was it with this woman? Why was she always hugging me? It was confusing. I couldn't possibly keep my careful mask in place, couldn't possibly act like Dawn Darkmore, if this woman was always treating me like...a person.

"Are you okay, dear?" The older woman pulled back, and our gazes met.

I stared. The older woman had such a kind face. Even though her hair was now weaved with pink, she made me wonder if this is what my grandmother would have been like.

But no. Grandmother was a Darkmore. Mother said she didn't hug. Rarely smiled. And that her expectations were even harsher than my own mother's.

"Dawn, dear?"

I shook myself back to reality, finding my throat strangely dry. "I'm fine."

Lucilla pushed the hair back from my face. "I'm going to be giving those Fates a talking-to. 'Stay out of it,' they said. But look what could have happened if Sabrina hadn't told us what was happening!"

"Really, I'm fine."

My great-aunt leaned closer. "It's all right to be in trouble sometimes, I promise. And when you need it, you have people here to help you take care of it."

I have people to take care of me? I mulled the thought over for a second, then dismissed it. *I don't need others to take care of me.* "Thank you," I said anyway.

Lucilla stared for a moment longer, then shook her head. "Let's go inside."

"Actually," Aiden said, the word stiff. "I think we should get out of here as fast as possible. Those warlocks are still tracking us."

"Boy," the police officer said, placing a firm hand on his shoulder. "You're not going anywhere until we talk. And my first question will be what the devil those creatures were that chased us, because they sure as hell weren't wolves."

Aiden's jaw worked, and for one long second I thought he would argue, but then he simply said, "Yes, sir."

"And I think I'm going to get going..." Sabrina inched back toward a beat-up truck.

I resisted the urge to call her a traitorous coward, after all, she'd sent Paul to help, so she hadn't completely abandoned us. I forced a smile instead. "Safe travels!"

Sabrina sent me an uncertain look, then fled.

Inside, the cabin smelled like chili again.

"I reheated it in my Crock-Pot," Lucilla said, proudly. "And it always tastes better the second day." She winked.

We all sat at the table and ate slowly. To my surprise, it was delicious. For the first time, it occurred to me how long it'd been since I ate a real meal. I picked at things. Drank the blood from the blood bank. But when was the last time I enjoyed a real meal?

Before Liam died. He'd always loved food.

I closed my eyes, and my spoon clattered into my half-empty bowl. How could I possibly sit here enjoying a meal when my brother was dead? When our family lands were in question? *What's wrong with me? I need to take my champion back and save what my brother worked so hard to build.*

"Is it good?" Lucilla asked, her dark brown eyes staring too intently.

"Delicious." I tried to keep eating, but the food tasted of ash.

Lucilla shook her head, her eyes too knowing.

Beside her, Aiden was on his second bowl.

"You like it?" Paul asked, his voice filled with pride.

"Yeah," he spoke around a mouthful of food. "Best thing I've ever had."

An unexpected grin spread the police officer's normally serious face. "The boy's got good taste."

Lucilla rolled her eyes. "He's a wounded, half-starved shifter. He'd eat the couch if we put some salt on it."

Paul's face changed to a serious one. "But is he? He smelled a bit different to me, but I couldn't quite put my finger on it. And then I just had a pack of 'wolves' shift into mutant dragon-birds."

My aunt's gaze swung to Aiden.

He put down his spoon and straightened, looking right back at her. "This is going to sound crazy, ma'am, but they aren't werewolves...they're warlocks." He paused, then pressed on as if afraid to be stopped. "They're criminals hiding out in our realm. They crashed their ship and since then have been experimenting on humans to create warlock hybrids. I was their first successful experiment. There's one more. Now that they have us, all they have to do is contact their leaders to get off this rock. Then, they'll set up a whole operation, changing human after human into hybrids. Using us for whatever they want, soldiers in their war, or breeders."

When he was finished, his eyes flashed with a challenge. Daring them not to believe him.

"So, you're telling me you can shift into a dragon-bird?" the police officer asked.

"No, as a hybrid, I can only shift into a wolf. I have no idea what their limits are."

"What can we do to stop this?" Lucilla broke in.

His jaw dropped open, but he quickly recovered. "You believe me?"

She laughed. "Of course, honey. Do you think this is our first warlock?"

Paul chuckled. "Not even close."

"We've even dealt with warlock schemes before."

Aiden stared at them silently, his disbelief and relief clearly evident in his expression. His mouth opened, then closed.

Lucilla turned to me. "Will he be okay?"

I felt my mouth curl into a smile. "I'm used to magical creatures, and I was still shocked about the warlocks. I think knowing the truth, and having people believe him, is a lot for him to take."

Lucilla nodded seriously at him. "Of course, honey. You take all the time you need."

The police officer harrumphed. "But the boy did say he needed to get out of here in a hurry."

Aiden seemed to come back to himself. "Yes, we do. The device I have can be used to communicate with the warlocks. There will be a ship passing through our realm on the night of the eclipse. If I can get in touch with the right people, I can stop all of this." Then, he looked at me. "And between then and now, I have to do something for Dawn in return for helping me."

"Sounds like you have a lot to do," Lucilla said with a smile.

We do, but...

I sat up straighter. "The thing is...my car is still in the middle of the desert."

My great-aunt's eyes twinkled like a mischievous teenager. "A little magic will help with that."

I took in the people and the atmosphere in the room and felt an unexpected wave of contentment. I might soon be facing the most difficult challenge of my life, but for the first time in longer than I could remember, I had a strange sense of certainty that everything would be okay.

It's this place. Ghost Town. It makes everything seem possible.

My aunt Lucilla reached across the table and took my hand. "Everything is happening just the way it's supposed to. I promise you."

That was hard to believe, but my gaze went to where her hand touched mine, and the question spilled out before I could stop it. "Why aren't you afraid to touch me? You know what I did. You know what I'm capable of. My whole life everyone has been afraid of me."

She smiled and squeezed my hand. "In a world where everyone is different, many of us have dark sides. Dangerous sides that we can't help. That doesn't mean that we don't deserve love or understanding. In your case, it just means no one should be touching you when you're terrified or angry. That's just who you are. It's not a choice. And anyone who cares about you will understand that."

"But my powers aren't just dangerous. They *kill*."

"But your other powers are just as important. Your power to be kind, to help those in needs, to protect your people. Those are all parts of you too, and if people can't take your edges, then they don't drive your softer side."

I disagreed. "People are right to fear me."

"And to love you," she told me, so easily that I almost believed her. "One day you'll be surrounded by friends and a lover who understands that."

"I don't think so," my voice sounded strangely weak, and I avoided Aiden's glance.

My aunt's smile never faltered. "I know you will. Even if you don't have faith in yourself right now, have faith in me."

"I'll try." But the truth was that after I left this town, I'd lose everyone who seemed to care about me. Not Aiden, at first, but him too, eventually.

I felt ice slide down my spine. *Today I returned to Mist. I stopped being Dawn and started being a Darkmore again.* Just the thought left me feeling oddly hollow.

17

DAWN

HALF AN HOUR LATER, I had changed out of my blood-soaked dress and into my high-waisted black pants, white lace shirt, and black boots. Regarding my reflection in the mirror, I pondered whether the shirt was too much. It was see-through, but in the most fashionable way possible, with an intricate, large circles design, and a modern, high neckline. It was classically beautiful and made by a genius designer, conforming to my curves. My black bra peeked out from beneath.

But paired with my loose bun, no one could find fault in it, and after a moment, I smiled at my reflection. Dawn Darkmore looked flawless.

Then my smile faltered. *Is this what the rest of my life is to be? To forever embody a leader—play the part? Is there anything inside me that remains that's just Dawn?*

I thought of Aiden. He made me feel like just Dawn. Too bad it would have been selfish beyond words to pursue him romantically in any way. Because one day my magic could come back and take his life, just as it had with my parents.

So, perhaps, this small time with him I can just be Dawn. I can pretend. As long as I keep a careful line between us.

There was a soft knocking at the bathroom door. "The car's back," Aiden called from the other side. "It...uh...flew here and landed in the driveway just a couple of minutes ago."

Magic definitely has its benefits...if only my powers were fun instead of dangerous.

I glanced at myself in the mirror one last time, turned, and opened the door.

His eyes widened as they fell on me, and then slid downward, stopping at my see-through shirt.

Even though I'd worn the classic outfit many times before, my cheeks heated. The desire in Aiden's gaze made me feel like I was dressed in nothing but a tiny pair of panties and a bra.

My gaze slid to his neck, my vampiric desires overtaking me again. What would it feel like to saunter up to him? To bite softly into the side of his neck? He would react immediately to my bite. I could just picture him, pulling me closer, and me wrapping my legs around his waist.

His cock would be hard. I knew plenty of shifters, and they were always hard. Always ready to go. Was a hybrid like him similar? I'd never slept with one myself, but from what I understood, they could go all night. And I would be more than willing to ride Aiden, bringing us both to climax over and over again. I shook the vision away.

He ran a hand through his dark hair and turned away from me. "I've been trying to figure out the communicator."

"Oh?" Everything was packed up. Everything except the

communicator on the table and the pages of notes Aiden had been scribbling. "Did you learn anything?"

He sat down. "I think so. Now, I'm not 100% sure, but I knew a ship would be passing between realms soon." He clicked on the device and pointed to a red dot, and then what looked like a veil. "I think we're five to six days out from when this ship will pass through our realm. Based on what I've charted out, it should be passing near, or in Mist, which tells me it's either the ship with the warlock's master, or the Magic Police have figured out at least the general area their escaped prisoners went to."

"Is there a way to know who it'll be?" I asked, not liking the idea of our enemies' boss showing up in my lands.

He shook his head. "What's more, I'm just taking an educated guess on when it will arrive. I'll have to keep monitoring it to be sure."

I let out a rush of breath. "Okay, then. That should still give us enough time to take care of both our problems."

"But we should hurry." His voice was gruff, but could I hear a trace of desire? Is that why he'd run over here and changed the subject?

A shiver ran down my spine. Maybe I was imagining it, but I didn't care.

At the door, he picked up my small bag and medical kit and strode outside. The early afternoon light and heat of the desert made me pause in the doorway. Lucilla and Officer Paul were chatting, laughing together by my car. It was strange because, at that moment, I realized there was more going on between them than just a friendship. And the thought of them having a chance at love made my heart glow.

I've spent only a little time with them, but it's strange how much I'm going to miss them. I swallowed around the lump in my throat.

Aiden opened the back of the car, and much to everyone's surprise, two lizards shot out.

"What in the—?" I couldn't believe it. *Lizards?*

Lucilla put her hands on her hips. "Boys!"

An instant later, the two lizards turned into twin boys. My distant cousins. They might not have been around the last time I visited, but I recognized them immediately from their pictures.

"What were you doing in the back of my car?" I searched my mind for any logical explanation and came up empty.

They stared down guiltily at their shoes. The taller blond-haired boy spoke first. "We overheard you guys going on some kind of hunt for something missing. It sounded fun, so we decided to tag along."

I shook my head. *Was I ever this reckless at their age?* "Do you realize how dangerous that was? Something really bad could have happened to you."

They nodded, and then the shorter one spoke. "We realized it after those things shifted into tiny dragon-birds, and Officer Paul had to save you. But you should know. After you left, someone pulled up behind your car. At first we could only hear him, not see him, but then his car suddenly became visible. We think he's following you."

"Did he see you?" Lucilla asked, her brow furrowed with worry.

"Don't worry, Aunty, we had it covered," the taller one said.

Lucilla's frown of worry deepened slightly, but she was silent.

My stomach sank. "Was he a vampire?"

The boy frowned. "No, definitely a shifter. But he called someone to say he'd lost track of you."

Draven.

Why did I think that? What could he have to do with warlock shifters in Ghost Town, Arizona?

Either my imagination was working overtime, or the fae blood from my mother's side was making connections for me again.

"Don't worry," Lucilla said, putting a hand on each of the twins' shoulders. "I'll take care of them. You guys head on your way."

I wanted to say more, but the words caught on my tongue.

And then, my great-aunt's arms were around me, squeezing me tightly once more.

Hesitantly, I reached out and hugged her back.

"You take care." Lucilla pulled back and gazed into my eyes. "And you should know, I called those distant relatives of ours, the Fates, and I told them I'd had just about enough of their nonsense. That you deserve something good."

I frowned. *Am I really related to the Fates?* I must have missed that branch of the family tree.

Aiden threw my bags into the back of the car and closed the door. He and Paul shook hands, exchanged a few mumbled words, and then all eyes were on me.

"Okay then," I said. "I guess it's time for us to go."

Lucilla and Paul headed for their truck, and Aiden and I moved closer, wanting to see them off. But just as my aunt was about to close her car door, Lucilla called after me. "And use that cream on him every night, or he won't be in shape in time for the big battle."

I nodded.

And then, my great-aunt looked between me and Aiden.

"And remember, it only works when a fae applies it. She will need to rub it into your skin every night if she wants you in fighting shape." She winked at us both. "I'm sure neither of you kids will mind all that much."

My cheeks felt hot as we watched them drive away, and then I avoided Aiden's gaze as we got back into my car. You know the only thing worse than having a crush on a guy you couldn't be with? Having someone point it out for everyone to see? But, I knew, my aunt was only trying to help. She didn't have a mean bone in her body.

I started the engine, trying my best not to make eye contact with the man in the seat next to me. *What must he be thinking of me and my family?*

And then I realized I didn't care. *I love them, and that's enough.*

The drive out of Ghost Town, Arizona was one of the hardest trips of my life. Because even though I knew I was headed back home, my eyes kept swinging back to the rearview mirror. Could Mist ever feel like Ghost Town?

It was a strange thought. I'd known I wanted to continue my brother's legacy, my family legacy. To continue building on the strong foundation of a city where magical people and humans could coexist. But perhaps...perhaps there was even more I could do. Maybe there was a way to do more than coexist with the other races.

Maybe we could all live happily together.

For the first time since my brother's death, I felt a spark of hope when I thought of my responsibilities. There was so much good I could do. *As long as I can defeat Draven.*

Glancing at Aiden, who was staring down at the communications device in his hand, I took a deep breath. "Is it a good time to talk about being my champion?"

He nodded, his gaze locking with mine. "Sure."

I tightened my grip on the steering wheel. *Where to start?* "Do you know why I need your help?"

"You need me to fight for you because someone wants your position."

"Yes." I paused. "But there's something you should know."

He stared, waiting.

"I used to be able to kill with a touch. All I had to do was want someone dead, touch them, and it happened. Or even just feel uncontrollably angry or upset and touch someone."

He didn't look the least bit surprised. *Of course.* "So why don't your powers work anymore?"

Damn it. I forced myself to keep breathing. I should have expected the question. And the answer still shouldn't hurt so deeply. It had been over a decade.

"There was a rebellion in Mist ten years ago. The supernatural creatures who were tired of vampires ruling without limits got tired of it." I squeezed the steering wheel, commanding my hands to stop shaking. "Our castle was overwhelmed with enemies. I'd been asleep. And suddenly, I was being attacked from every direction. Shifters, trolls, goblins, and fae, they all came at me."

I focused on the road ahead of me, terrified that the memories would sweep me under. "I used my powers over and over again, killing everyone who touched me before they could hurt me. Someone touched my shoulders from behind. I turned and reached out...it was both my parents, one on each side. They'd come to help. And I...I..." My mouth opened and closed, but the words wouldn't come out.

He took one of my hands from the steering wheel and closed it in his warm ones. Without a word, he reassured me. Without a word, he touched me, unafraid even after knowing what I'd done.

After a long moment, I cleared my throat and continued, "Anyway, my powers disappeared that night and haven't returned since."

"And now your brother has died," he said, softly.

I nodded. "Without my powers, I need you to fight in my place. But Draven—the one against me—he's a very powerful vampire and a fire elementalist. I'm not sure if you can—"

"I'll defeat him."

I glanced at him. "You sound so confident."

He shrugged. "That's because I am."

"Men," I said, laughing. "None of you ever have a short supply of arrogance."

The corners of his mouth lifted into an almost-smile. "It isn't arrogance. I just have no problem destroying anyone who threatens you."

My laughter died, and I felt a strange warmth in my chest. "You really mean that, don't you?"

His expression grew serious. "Of course."

And for some reason, the fact that I believed him made me feel even worse.

Does he really know what he's up against?

What have I gotten him into?

18

AIDEN

THE TRIP to Mist would have taken far longer for a human. But Dawn drove the Bentley like the hounds of hell were chasing her, sipping lukewarm blood she'd pulled out of a small cooler in her bag, driving a full day without rest.

I watched her with fascination. It was strange how she could be both the popular human girl I knew back in school and a vampire. I almost wouldn't have believed the vampire bit, if not for the blood she poured into the glass in her cup holder. *And if you weren't a warlock hybrid shifter yourself,* I thought mirthlessly.

But there were traces of that girl in the woman in front of me, in her smile, her wit, her confidence. I never would have expected how comfortable I felt with her. She talked about her family, her mansion, and her lands, always with a mixture of pride and obligation.

She asked me about my time in the warlock labs too. I gave her the PG-13 version of what they had done to me, and she listened with avid interest. I'd almost thought she was so used to death and pain that it didn't impact her, but then she'd turned to me with cold eyes and said, "I'm going to kill those warlocks if I ever see them again."

Should I have been aroused by her words? Probably not. But hell if my body cared.

It wasn't until we slowed as we passed an ancient-looking sign that read Welcome to Mist that Dawn grew quiet. Her knuckles gripping the steering wheel turned white, and she held herself rigidly in her seat. I felt a similar tension. This is where I'd grown up. Where I'd spent my time being abused by my foster father, ignored by most people, and eventually been kidnapped from. And yet, it was the tension in her body that bothered me, not my own.

"Are you okay?"

She took a long time to answer. "Of course."

I tilted my head, telling myself to be quiet even while I started talking. "You do that a lot."

"What?" She glanced at me, the afternoon sun washing her in its beautiful light.

"Say you're fine when you clearly aren't."

She opened her mouth, a look of frustration written across her face, but then closed it. Her expression fell. "What else should I say? The truth? I'm a leader, Aiden. Leaders aren't people, as my mother said over and over again. People don't want to see our inner struggles. They equate it with weakness. They want to see us as calm, confident, and capable."

"Maybe you have to be that way in front of your people, but you don't have to be that way in private. With the people who care for you."

She turned back to face the road, but I could see moisture in her eyes. And I could practically hear the wheels turning in her mind. "My brother was the perfect ruler in front of our people. No one knew how silly he was. How he would mess up my hair every chance he could get. How he made the corniest jokes imaginable." She smiled even as a tear rolled down her cheek. "I could be myself with him. But now...there's no one else I can let my guard down with."

I felt a deep ache in my chest. "You can let your guard down with me."

She shook her head, another tear rolling down her cheek. "After this is done, you'll be gone."

"Only if you want me to be." My words seemed to hang between us. *What did I just say?*

"Aiden..." She took a deep breath. "You know I'm not safe, right? My powers, they're gone right now, but what if they come back?"

"You think being a weird warlock shifter doesn't have its risks?" I tried to sound playful, but my tone was serious.

She slowed the car at the first red light outside the town. "With how dangerous I am, you should put distance between us when this is done."

I clenched my fists. "I know I should...but if you wanted me to remain by your side, I would. In whatever capacity that you wanted me."

The light turned green, and she slowly sped up. The car felt strangely silent after our nearly twenty-four hours of constant chatter. At last, she looked at me, her stunning hazel eyes full of emotion. "But you could be free. You grew up with a foster father who is dead, and then you were taken by those warlock bastards. Once you are done being my champion, you have the whole world before you."

My throat closed. "I never thought that far ahead." I turned the communications device over in my hand. "I honestly just wanted to survive long enough to send the message. I figured I'd be dead not long after."

"But now you'll send the message and live," she emphasized.

It was strange how hollow I felt as I told her the truth. "I don't have family. I don't have friends. Or a career. Or a home. So, I guess I don't know what I'll do."

"Well, I do." Her chin lifted as she spoke. "My head of security needs to retire. I'll have him train you, and you'll take over for him. After being my champion, you should want for nothing. If you want to stay, then Darkmore will be your home. Forever."

I stared at her for a long moment as I mulled her words over. Her offer was...kind and generous. But it was obviously not made with romantic intentions. Could I ever live with Dawn without being *with* her? The idea made me feel like those damn warlocks were experimenting on me again. Somewhere in the region of my heart.

"I'll think about it."

But instead of thinking about her offer, I was thinking about what it would take to convince her that I was safe with her. That if she wanted me, I would be hers in an instant. *I'll find a way. If she'll accept me for the freak I am, then I'll do everything in my power to win her over.*

We didn't talk for the remainder of the trip. Instead, I stared out at a town that looked as different from Ghost Town, Arizona as I could imagine. The landscape was lush, overflowing with massive trees covered in orange, red, and yellow leaves. There was a strong element of something not quite right. *Why didn't I pick up on that in all the years I lived here?*

And that's when I realized it. *There's magic everywhere!* Humans and magical beings walked side by side on the street. A dwarf scurried along, glaring down at a paper in his hands. Three young fairies who glowed slightly giggled together. And an angry-looking shifter stepped out of a coffee shop, a brief flash of yellow in his eyes as he glared down at his drink.

"Why are all these creatures out in broad daylight? Aren't they afraid of being seen?"

Dawn turned to me and laughed. "That's right. You aren't human anymore. The glamour doesn't work on you."

I frowned. "What glamour?"

She laughed. "The humans here don't know what we are. And it takes a lot of power to keep all the magical beings hidden from them. To live among them without being discovered by them. This is supposed to be a town without supernaturals. If the government ever found out we were here, we'd be in trouble."

"So it was this full of supernaturals when I lived here?"

She grinned. "Of course."

"And that's why this place is so special?"

Her smile faltered, and her beautiful hazel eyes lost a bit of their shine. "Darkmore was built on ancient lands used to bury the bodies of magical creatures. Liam and I discovered that the ghosts here carry enough residual magic to use to cast a glamour over the land. That's also why Draven wants our lands so badly. I can't rule from anywhere else—or I could, but the humans would know what I am, and the government would control everything we do. Draven wants these lands, but the ghosts...they won't obey anyone but the head of our coven."

I turned back to the buildings. They had an old-time charm, even though many of them looked recently built. But far from being innocent and welcoming, the town had a darker feel to it than Ghost Town, darker than the many places I'd raced through since escaping the warlock shifters.

It had never occurred to me how I would go about surviving in this world where I was a freak, where the government would probably love to get its hands on me. I would have to hide who I was. That was, anywhere but here.

"This place is important," she announced softly. "My people deserve to live somewhere safe. But if Draven takes control, it won't be safe anymore. He'll try to change it back to a system where vampires ruled entirely. He'll feed on any creature he wants, kill, and use the other magical beings as little more than slaves. And because these people won't want to leave Mist, there will be another civil war. And this time, my brother isn't around to stop it."

She cares about this place and these people. "Then, we'll stop him."

She smiled. "I wish I felt as confident as you do."

"That's probably because you haven't seen what I can do when I'm not a battered mess." I smiled wryly.

One of her brows rose. "About that. We need to make sure I put that cream they gave us on you every night. I know you feel confident, but Draven is cruel. He doesn't follow any rules, and he's powerful. We need you at your best."

An image of her rubbing cream on me ran through my mind, and I had to bite back a groan that had nothing to do with me getting well. "Whatever you think is best."

Just on the other side of town, we turned onto a short, paved road crowded by large trees. Outside the city, the mist grew and grew. And within a short drive, it lay heavy over the ground.

My eyes narrowed as I gazed at the mist more carefully. "Are those...ghosts?"

She smiled. "You bet."

I shook my head. Being a part of this paranormal world was going to take some getting used to. I'd lived in this town until I was taken and never thought there was anything strange about the mist. In fact, as much as I'd noticed a division between the poor and wealthy, I'd never suspected anything supernatural about anyone. It seemed that a town that claimed to be only for humans would simply only have humans.

What a fool I'd been.

After a short drive, we came to a massive set of black iron gates. In the middle of the two gates was a huge cursive *D*.

She unrolled her window as she came to a guard post on one side.

A vampire dressed in a black uniform took one step out of the tiny building, and his eyes widened. "Lady Darkmore!"

He stepped back inside, and seconds later, the towering gates opened.

We continued on a straight path lined by well-trimmed trees and sculpted bushes. Even the flowers seemed to be in their proper places. Halfway down the road, the trees stopped. In front of us were acres and acres of short, bright green grass that stretched out until reaching a dark manor.

She drove her Bentley down the road and came to a stop on the circular drive. "Time to face the music," she mumbled to herself, then cut the engine.

We both got out of the car.

A second later, a butler in a crisp uniform stepped out of one of the towering front doors.

"Henry, assemble the staff," Dawn ordered, grabbing a knee-length white jacket from the trunk of the car and buttoning it over her wrinkled clothing. For the first time, I saw the woman who would lead these people.

Staff in black-and-white uniforms poured out of the two enormous front doors, lining up along the sidewalk just in front of her car. More staff came from the back of the house. Within moments, thirty people waited, standing rigid.

She let her gaze run over all of them before speaking. "My brother, the great Liam Darkmore, will be forever missed. No one can replace him, and yet, I am the last remaining Darkmore. You have served my brother well over your lifetime, as did your ancestors before you, and I know that you will serve me well too."

Several nods of assent greeted her announcement.

"You should also know that in good times or in bad, we will stick together. I will protect you, just as my family before me." Her hands formed into fists. "But as much as I want us to be in a good time at the beginning of my rule, these times are not safe. We should be prepared for anything in the days to come. I want you to be on high alert. If you see anything suspicious, report it to Halloway at once."

The butler spoke with some hesitation. "Is there something we should be concerned with?"

She answered as if she'd practiced many times. "Everything will be revealed in due time. Until then, be alert, but not afraid. There is no reason for anyone on my staff to ever be afraid."

At this, the servants stood straighter.

Her back rigid, Dawn started up the small staircase leading to the door. Two men scrambled to open the doors before she reached them. At the top of the stairs, she paused and the bottom of her jacket swirled as she turned back to look at me. "Coming?"

I hurried after her, barely making it inside the huge doors before the staff rushed in after me.

She turned back to them, and I felt like I was in another world as they swarmed her, welcoming her home, awaiting orders. She gave them instructions. Where to put her suitcases. Where to set up my room. When dinner should be prepared. For a tailor to take my measurements and bring me clothes immediately. For security to be increased around the city and around her home. And, finally, arranging a time for her to meet with the head of security, Halloway, privately. Through it all, she was calm, patient, reassuring.

When all the orders were given, she turned and motioned for me to follow her down a quiet hall. She stopped at a simple door, glancing behind me. "We will be having refreshments in my office. Please come get me when everything has been taken care of."

I realized that an older vampire with auburn hair had followed us. The man gave an easy smile, nodded, and hurried away.

Then, Dawn looked back at me. "Shall we?"

I followed her into the office, but my steps felt heavy. It was one thing to know Dawn was rich, powerful, and well beyond my reach. It was another thing to see it firsthand.

After I've fought for her, I can't remain. These people would never accept me as their leader. And I...I have no knowledge of these things. I would only bring her down.

In the plush office, with its roaring fire and walls of books, we discussed the days to come. We tried to use the communications device again. I turned it on, created a message, and streamed it out into space. The device confirmed what I already knew. There were no ships close enough to receive the message.

I turned it off, not wanting to waste the battery. *Three*

days until the eclipse, then the message can be sent, and this can be done, once and for all.

It was hard to still have the task hanging over me, but nothing was harder than having Dawn so close, but not being able to touch her.

That was its own kind of torture.

19

DAWN

I STARED at the invitation on my vanity.

DEAR LADY DARKMORE,

Your presence is requested at the residence of Lord Draven Cerberus for a celebration of the life of Liam Darkmore. This evening promptly at nine o'clock.

MY DEEPEST REGARDS,
Lord Cerberus

I CRUMPLED the invitation in my hand, breathing hard, overwhelmed with emotion. *That pathetic weasel would challenge me tonight —my first night back.*

There was no other reason for such an event. But if he

thought that he would find me unprepared, he would soon learn how truly wrong he was.

He will ask me to select a day for our battle. I must fight for enough time for Aiden to heal.

My narrowed gaze moved up to my reflection in the mirror. My pale hair had been pulled up into a simple, elegant bun. The shoulderless gown was made of a dark red lace the color of blood, which matched the subtle streaks of red in my hair. The dress clung to every curve of my body like a web. It was simple but striking. No one in the room would dare to argue that I wasn't a Darkmore, through and through.

"The Darkmores are like a simple, well-made blade. No one could look at us without knowing we're dangerous." I spoke my father's words, my canines lengthening in the mirror.

Yes, Aiden was my champion because of my lack of magic and because of the prophecy, but I would not allow such a thing to cripple me. I would not let a single person know how vulnerable I felt.

Someone knocked at my door.

I gathered my long skirt in my hand and stood on my one-of-a-kind shoes, a deep gold that complimented the gown perfectly. Taking two steps forward, I smoothed my skirt, sliding my shaking hands along the tight bodice. "Come in."

Aiden entered, and I forgot to breathe.

God, no man should be able to look so hot.

He wore a tux that looked like a second skin. It clung to his wide shoulders and buttoned perfectly at his trim waist. I had seen many men in tuxes over the years, but none had fit the man like this one fit Aiden. Every part of him screamed *male*.

My gaze rose to his face. He'd left his scruffy beard, although he'd trimmed it to be less scruffy. Which I liked. *Too much.* His hair had been cut too, a little long on top and short on the sides. It was styled perfectly, emphasizing the cut of his jaw and drawing attention to eyes so blue they were breathtaking.

"You look incredible," he said.

I swallowed hard, my heart racing. "You too."

He seemed unsure, hovering in my doorway. And so, I took his elbow rather than waiting for him to hold it out for me. I could lead him through the customs of the night. "There's nothing for you to be nervous about, you know. We both know the challenge will be given. This is all a dance. Politics." And politics I could handle.

He made a noncommittal noise and led me down the stairs and out to the waiting car.

"A Lexus limousine?" Aiden turned to me, his brows raised.

I shrugged. "I never even noticed."

The driver opened the door for me, and I slid in, conscious of his eyes on me. Immediately, I closed the screen between us and the driver, and turned to Aiden, placing a hand on his knee. "I didn't get to ask this before, but are you all right with going back onto Draven's lands? I know that's where they held you." *What must it be like for him to go back to the place where he was tortured, experimented on by those warlock shifters?* Suddenly I stilled. *Are my lands worth this?*

Aiden tensed. "I don't think any of the Shadow Keepers will be here tonight."

"Yes, but, I feel like you've been through enough, trying to get the communicator to save the humans. And now I'm sacrificing your safety for the safety of my people." I studied my hands. "It doesn't feel right."

He gave a sad chuckle. "The good of the many versus the good of the one, right?"

That's how I've always felt. Suddenly, I saw Aiden in a new light. *Perhaps we are more alike than I could have thought.* "You seem nervous."

His knee jerked beneath my touch. "Perhaps a bit."

I smiled. "You know you don't actually have to fight tonight."

His eyes widened. "I know that. It's just...I spent the afternoon talking to Halloway and your security detail. They'll be everywhere, but Halloway made it very clear that my priority is to act as your escort. To watch for anything that could harm you. That, I can do." He took a deep breath. "But I've never been to something like this before, and with vampires no less. I'm going to screw up and embarrass you somehow. I know it," he admitted.

I squeezed his knee. "Aiden, look at me."

Hesitantly, he looked at me.

"There's nothing you can do to embarrass me. The people who love my family won't care what rules of etiquette you break. And the assholes who are waiting for us to screw up, well, who cares what they think?"

One corner of his mouth lifted. "You truly are incredible."

I leaned back, looking out the window. "Yes, I'm one of a kind, all right." *More like the last of my kind. But I will not let him defeat me.*

The drive felt too long and too short all at once when we finally turned to the right and entered Draven Cerebrus's territory. The headlights bounced along the road and reflected off the darkened trees around us. In the shadows, I knew, my vampire security detail was racing to take their places according to whatever plan Halloway had determined. But even though my senses seemed to be stretching out all around me, my gaze swung back to Aiden and remained.

"No," he said, reading my mind. "I'm fine. It's just...I was hiking in these woods when they caught me. And for years, they only let me see the sun when they 'practiced' with me out here. When they hunted me. When they taught me to shift. It's...strange to be back."

Those sick bastards. "Don't worry about them, because if I see them again, I'm going to kill them."

Aiden laughed. "Wouldn't that be nice?"

"No," I said. "I mean it. Part of being a supernatural creature is using your strength to protect the weak. If I see those things again, their blood will run." My teeth ground together as I tried to gain a hold of the rush of anger that came at the thought of Aiden being hurt.

"I'm not weak," he said, softly.

I turned to him, noting each conflicting emotion as it raced across his face. *He thinks I'm doubting him as a man.* "You're not weak...I didn't mean that. I just want them to pay for what they did to you, and I want to make sure they never hurt another innocent again."

My words were met with silence, and then, after a moment he spoke slowly. "Did you have anything to do with my foster father going missing?"

I stiffened, shocked by the question. Unsure of my response. *Will he hate me for what I did? Fear me?* I clenched my hands. It didn't matter how he might react, he deserved to know the truth. To fully understand what I was. "I killed him. That night I picked you up in my car. And I did it slowly. Painfully."

He nodded. "I thought so. Thank you."

Thank you? The relief I felt almost made me laugh. "I thought you might be upset."

He shrugged. "I hated that man." He paused. "However badly you think he hurt me. It was much, much worse. For years and years. And I wasn't the first. A man like him shouldn't get to live. Shouldn't get to keep hurting children for a government paycheck."

"Oh, Aiden…" I wanted to tell him I was sorry. That what happened to him was wrong. But something about the way he held himself made me swallow the words. *This isn't the time.*

We broke through the thick woods that surrounded the road. In front of us, a dark castle was nearly overwhelmed by trees and plants left wild. Sickly green vines covered the bottom half of the building as if attempting to take the land for the wilderness once more. Dozens of expensive vehicles were already parked on the other side of the circular driveway.

"Looks like we're the last to arrive," I said, wishing my palms weren't so sweaty.

"Is that good or bad?"

Bad. "It doesn't matter. A Darkmore can never be anything but fashionably late." *Layla said the vote will be split. The fact that he had the other houses come before me won't change that.*

"So, we're ready?" he asked.

I released a slow breath. "Yeah. We're ready."

20

Dawn

Our car stopped as close to the building as it could get. The driver ran around swiftly and opened the door, and I exited in grand fashion. I swept my long skirts so that they would flow evenly around me, then took Aiden's arm. *We can do this. I won't lose my family's home and everything we fought so hard for. I will protect my people.*

I will.

At the top of the stairs, the doors were open. Music exploded out into the cool, quiet night. It was harsh, angry music. Something that suited Draven Cerberus perfectly.

We entered the hall, and I felt every muscle in Aiden's arm tighten. On both sides of our path alcoves with beds had curtains pulled back. Feeders stood in some of the open doorways, barely clothed. They showed their necks, which already had far too many unhealed bite marks on them, and gestured for us to join in.

I shook my head and pulled Aiden along, who stared, his jaw tightened with anger. Growls and moans came from the next room. I caught sight of a human female and two vampire males in bed out of the corner of my eye, but didn't turn my face toward them, simply continued into the main part of the house.

Feeders were approved by my brother, but this is not how they handled these people in my home. Instead, humans and magical creatures were active parts of my household, and when I was hurt, or in dire need of fresh blood, I used them with respect.

We don't treat our Feeders like pieces of meat or livestock.

Perhaps harsher rules on the treatment of these people will be one of my first orders of business.

"I've never seen vampires eat before," Aiden whispered softly in my ear. "Is this how it always is?"

I shook my head. "No. Not even close."

Another set of doors was opened into a chaotic party. The room was dark other than red lights that flashed in random order around the room. Women danced, barely clothed, in cages that hung from the ceiling. And most of the massive space was crowded with dancing bodies.

At the far end of the room, Draven sat on a gray throne, human women surrounding him. Rubbing against him. One writhed in his lap as he regarded her, fangs bared.

I gritted my teeth. "So this is how you honor my brother?!" my voice boomed through the room.

As I entered, slowly, regally, humans and vampires turned to stare. Their dancing slowed and then stopped. After a moment, the angry music stopped too, and normal lights brightened slightly along the walls.

"Dawn!" Draven shouted from across the now-silent room. "Come in! Join the celebration!"

Aiden squeezed my hand softly in reassurance. I squeezed back, then let go of his elbow, my strides lengthening.

The crowd parted at my approach. When I reached the bottom of the stairs of his throne, I continued on until I was standing two feet in front of Draven.

"You will address me as Lady Darkmore." My voice cut through the quiet room like a knife. "My family has ruled these lands for hundreds of years, and you will respect it."

He rose, the red-and-orange light in his eyes danced with his elementalist magic. "I thought to give you time to enjoy the celebration, but—"

"This celebration is over. It is not fitting to honor the life of my great brother with this...madness."

Fire sparked to life in his palm, but I didn't flinch away from it. "I'm sorry if it displeases you."

"Are you?" I cocked my head. "Because only a fool would think this celebration, one that flouts our laws and disrespects the humans of our lands, appropriate. Are you a fool, Draven?"

"That's Lord Cerberus to you." His words were clipped as he looked from me to the crowd behind me. "And I am no fool. A fool is a person who would challenge a person far more powerful than themselves."

I smiled, glancing at the crowd behind me. "It seems that my brother's passing has loosened Draven's tongue."

A laugh rose up from the people watching the exchange.

"What are you implying?" Draven asked, encroaching on my space.

I straightened to my full height, which was half a head shorter than the vampire who challenged me. "I am implying that you, Draven, are a coward. A man who held his tongue while my brother ruled, but who suddenly seems to have grown a spine." I placed one hand on my hip and looked back at the crowd. "Remember the story of good Lady Cynda? She fought an attack against an army of orcs using her power over the elements. When she was finished, she turned to her sister, who pierced her through the chest with a sword. Lady Serna called herself a hero for defeating the slayer of the orc army. But no one called her brave. She will forever be remembered in history as a coward. So now, *Lord* Cerberus, what would you say to me, while my brother's grave is still fresh?"

I felt it. Every eye in the room on the man near me. And in my people's gazes, I saw their mixed emotions. Some looked guilty. Others looked expectant.

Turning back to the man I despised, I waited.

It took him a few moments to recover, during which I saw the workings of his mind in the expressions on his face. Then I saw it, the second he decided to challenge me regardless of what their people thought of me. Or him.

"Lady Serna attacked a powerful woman who deserved to lead her people in a moment of weakness, driven by blind greed for a position she could not otherwise attain. I will not do that, Lady Darkmore." He gazed around the room, the orange fires in his eyes gleaming with unholy light. "Instead, I ask that the houses appoint me as leader of the coven, in absence of a family member of the Darkmore house worthy of leading us."

The crowd erupted into murmurs and shouts.

Lord Jareth Emrick came forward, separating himself from the crowd. He wore a well-tailored dark tux that emphasized his height and muscles. Unexpectedly, my gaze swung to Aiden who watched the situation through narrowed eyes. *Before I saw Aiden, I thought Jareth was the largest man alive.* Now, he looked almost normal-sized.

Jareth winked at me and crossed his arms over his broad chest. "My vote is with the Darkmore house. They have ruled us long and well, and I believe Lady Dawn will continue to do so."

Bacia Kyran shoved her way forward next, wearing a tight short black dress. "My vote is with the Cerberus house. We vampires are the top of the food chain." She sneered. "I think somehow we forgot that."

From one corner came a strong, deep voice. Lorcan Aldon stood from a chair in one corner, his bushy gray brows drawn low. He leaned heavily on a cane, his glare sweeping over the room. "The Darkmore house brought civility. Class. An age of peace and enjoyment of the finer things."

"Do you have a point, old man?" Draven shouted, clenching his jaw tightly.

Lord Aldon's gaze sharpened on my enemy. "My vote is with the Darkmore house. Not a spineless bastard."

The ball of flames in Draven's hand grew.

The old man inhaled sharply and blew. Air rushed through the room, knocking down the people in its path, and the flame in Draven's hand died. Insulting one of Lord Cynda's ancestors was a poor choice, even by the cocky vampire's standard.

Draven ran a shaking hand through his silver hair. "I— well, my vote of course is with the house of Cerberus. And as the rules state, the current leader of the coven cannot vote."

"So, a tie," Lord Aldon remarked.

I saw the sympathy in his pure silver eyes as he caught my gaze.

Draven's pleasure was written across his face. He stalked forward, faster than a human, and leaned into me, his breath whispering hot against my ear. "Agree to be my bride, and I will not challenge you to the customary fight."

I shoved him back, anger heating my blood. "I would rather die than share your bed!" I retorted loudly. Too loudly.

Murmurs rose behind me along with a few laughs. And then, like an explosion, everyone was laughing.

Draven's expression was thunderous. "Just for that, your death won't be quick." Then, he raised his voice. "House of Cerberus challenges House of Darkmore to a fight to the death. Winner take all."

The laughter died.

There was stillness.

They think I am defeated.

"House of Darkmore calls Aiden Cardon as its champion." I turned and looked at Aiden. He held his head high, his expression one of confidence, as he took a step forward and nodded.

My enemy's face twisted in disbelief. "A shifter? Is that what that thing is?" He laughed, a hollow sound filled with shock. "Wouldn't it be more merciful to kill him now?"

I smirked. "Careful, Draven, your fear is starting to show."

Murmurs went through the crowd.

"She can't be serious."

"He must not be a normal shifter."

"What is she doing?"

Turning my back on all of them, I started toward the door, Aiden following closely behind.

"The battle will be held in two days' time," Draven shouted at my back.

"A week," I said over my shoulder, not slowing.

"And here I thought to give him a chance. Aren't wolves strongest before the full moon?"

I stiffened. He was right. Why hadn't I thought about it? *Does it work the same with warlock shifters?* I glanced at Aiden. He gave me the subtlest nod.

I wanted to give him more time to heal. "Two days," I agreed, speaking loud enough for all to hear.

We strode past the Feeders and exited out to the coldness of night. At the bottom of the stairs, my car waited, expectantly. My driver opened the door at my approach. But just as I was about to climb in, a voice stopped me.

"Lady Darkmore!"

Lord Jareth Emrick was hurrying down the stairs. The clumsy movements of his large body made me appreciate Aiden's grace even more.

He smiled as he reached the bottom of the stairs, running a hand through his too-long blond hair. "May I speak to you a moment?"

I turned to Aiden and nodded.

Aiden stepped back, but only to the car, where he waited, his body tense. Alert.

"My lady." To my surprise, Jareth reached out and took my hand. His gentle brown eyes seemed to caress my face. "This is the last thing I wanted for you. In this time of grief, that monster strives to hurt you even more."

I forced a smile. Jareth was a good man. A vampire who had easily adapted to the changes in Mist. A man who hated violence and protected the weak without thought. "Thank you, Jareth. Your support meant the world to me."

"I'm glad." He moved closer to me. "The thing is, Dawn, I know things between us have never been more than friendship. But I'm growing tired of an empty house full of the memories of my dead family members, just as I'm sure you are. I'm not certain that I could defeat Draven in a fight, but I think I stand a better chance than your friend the shifter. So, I have a proposal for you. Be my bride. We could have a family together. And I believe with our joining, I can convince Bacia to side with us."

My mouth fell open with a gasp. I tried to speak, but no words came out. Jareth was a friend to me. I had never thought of him in a romantic way. But if marrying him could spare Aiden a battle that could take his life? *What should I do?*

"Before you answer," he said, "let me make my intentions clearer." And then, before I could react, he kissed me.

A second of pure surprise overtook me, and then I pulled back.

He smiled, a look I thought was meant to be sexy. *And it might have been. If not for a certain hybrid shifter behind me.*

"Think it over," Jareth said, turning and striding back to the party.

I slowly turned to Aiden, reluctant to see his reaction.

The agony in his face took my breath away. I hurried forward, reaching for him, but he moved out of my reach, and my hands fell.

Standing stiffly at my door, he didn't look at me. Instead, he motioned for me to climb in.

I did so with my heart in my throat.

He sat beside me. The chill from his body radiated, filling the tight space.

"Aiden—"

"Don't," he commanded, his voice low and threatening.

Not sure what else to do, I sat beside him in silence. Tears pricked the corners of my eyes. I knew if I spoke about Jareth's offer, he would tell me to refuse. I should keep my own counsel. Decide in the quiet of my room. But could I bear to let him think I was interested in another man? *Is being a Darkmore going to cost me the chance for love?*

Or hadn't my cursed powers already done that for me?

The drive to my home was one of the loneliest of my life.

21

Lord Draven Cerberus

MY TEETH CLENCHED together as the night's party continued all around me. Most of the important guests had left after Dawn's acceptance of my challenge. But while I expected this to be a night of enjoyment, the whole thing had left a bad taste in my mouth.

I'd never wanted Dawn dead. I just wanted her to accept me as her husband. Yes, it seemed only natural the stubborn woman would instinctively want to refuse my kind offer, but I'd thought she'd be smart enough to realize she had no choice.

And what the fuck was it with the shifter? Or whatever he was? Something about him felt off to me, but I couldn't quite place what it was. What was more, a shifter was about as capable of taking me on as she was, so why would she choose him as her champion? It made zero sense. As a vampire with control over the elements, it would be a slaughter.

Easy enough. I would win. I would take her house. And when she knew she had lost, she would agree to be my bride.

Well, only if she was scared enough. The bitch still seemed to think she was all-powerful. *That* would need to be addressed. Someone would need to remind her that she no longer had her touch of death.

I smiled. And I was just the one to do it.

Gesturing to my shifter, I sent the human females around me away. He approached, his expression tense as he leaned in close enough that we could talk without being overheard.

"I want you to go to her manor. I want you to hurt her. Not kill her. Just remind her that she too can feel pain. She too can suffer."

The shifter drew back from me, his dark eyes ringed by yellow, uncertain. "She is well protected there."

I lifted a brow. "Are you saying it can't be done?"

Very quickly, he shook his head. "It can be done."

"Then, stop wasting my time with this shit." He started to move away, when another thought occurred to me. "And what are your thoughts on that shifter?"

He paused before speaking, his long dark hair partially concealing his expression from my view. "He's not a shifter. He's something else. He smells like a wolf, only a very powerful wolf, higher than an alpha. I've never scented a creature like him before."

That wasn't good. But still, a beast was just a beast. They all cooked just as fast when I burned them to death.

"Go take care of my woman."

He bowed his head and took off out of the room. Sure, he was a better tracker than a killer, but I kept him around because he was useful. If ever he was caught, few people would believe that I would work with a shifter. It was my way of keeping my hands clean.

I caught Bacia Kyran's eye across the dance floor, where she'd been grinding against a human while drinking his blood. She pulled her teeth from the man's throat and shoved him onto the floor. I could also hear her hiss under her breath as she made her way toward me. I knew Bacia had backed me because she hoped when I became the coven leader I would marry her. It wasn't that I'd lied to her, I'd simply allowed her to believe what she wanted.

She had said we thought alike. That was true. We both wanted to stop this ridiculous shit in Mist and stop hiding in the shadows. They wanted a town only for humans? Well, that was too bad. They could stay right where they are and accept that they were our food source and that there wasn't a thing they could do to stop us.

Bacia comes to stop at the foot of my throne. "It was a good night."

"Was it?" I asked, lifting a brow.

She nodded. "You knew she left in search of a champion, and now we've seen her pathetic warrior. You'll defeat him with ease."

I lifted a hand and nudged my powers. A ball of flames formed in my hand, and I studied it. Bacia was right, the strange shifter would be easy to defeat, but something about him bothered me. Something I couldn't put my finger on. Maybe the same thing that my shifter had sensed in him.

And yet, I wasn't a shifter, so his smell couldn't have bothered me. So what was it?

"Did he look familiar to you?"

Bacia frowned, her expression thoughtful. "No, and I think I'm aware of all the shifters in Mist."

So was I, and I doubted he was just some random man who had passed through in the past. "Okay."

"Stop worrying," she said, with a wave of her hand. "Besides, aren't there some tasty treats in your dungeons?"

I stiffened. "How do you know about them?"

Bacia laughed. "I know about a lot of things, my dear. Now, shall we go enjoy the fruits of your labor?"

I hadn't wanted to share the humans I'd had my men kidnap, but since it was forbidden, and I didn't want Bacia tattling on me, I was left with few choices. So, I stood and offered her my arm. Together, we walked down to the dungeons where the delicious sounds of sobbing and screaming humans filled the air.

"Which one would you like?" I asked.

Her gaze darted to me. "And I can kill them? I don't have to save them?"

I grinned. "Of course."

She lifted a hand and pointed. "That one."

I snatched the keys to the cell doors and a thrill raced through me as my gaze met with one of the humans. Smiling, I whistled a tune as the woman inside began to scream and beg.

It was hard not to laugh. Did she realize that all her screaming and begging only served to turn me on? Probably not.

Bacia ran a hand down my arm. "And when we're done with them..."

Yes, I would fuck her. But it would mean nothing. Just a way to tame the fire within me before I won my bride and the position I so rightfully deserved.

Just two more days and I would have it all.

22

AIDEN

I STOOD on the balcony connected to my room, feeling empty. After dropping off Dawn in her suite, I'd taken a shower and put on a clean pair of boxers. A servant had dropped off a meal, which I ate even though the rich food tasted of nothing at all. Then, I checked the communicator. The damn ship still seemed to be about four days away, *if* I had figured the timing of when it would cross into our realm out, based on the little blinking dot that seemed to take a day to get through each line dividing it from us. Lines that I *assumed* represented the other realms. There were still four lines between us and the dot, so I was hoping I had the timing right.

Although understanding the technology from another realm wasn't exactly easy.

What was worse than not being sure about the exact day and time of something so important, I still didn't know whether that dot was the enemy ship, or the help I'd been looking for. After a while of staring at the device with frustration, I'd turned it off and ignored the damned thing. Frustrated, feeling like I didn't have control over anything, Now, I stared out at the woods that surrounded Dawn's manor, everything inside of me screaming.

If I hadn't just been through hell, I would've thought there was something wrong. An unknown danger surrounding us. But, I'd learned, my emotional state could sometimes make me feel this way, like something was wrong outside of me when the real problem was within.

Seeing Dawn kissed by another man was one of the worst moments of my life. The physical torture I'd endured at the hands of the warlocks at least had an end. I knew it couldn't go on forever. But this feeling? It echoed through me, slicing me over and over again. And I had a feeling it wasn't going to stop until my heart stopped beating.

Lord Jareth something or other was good-looking, young, wealthy, and of the same status as Dawn. Of course, she wanted him. That made sense. All my fantasies of her wanting a poor, broken freak? That made no sense at all.

I knew there couldn't be anything between us. Why did I let myself want her? I'm so stupid. I'm here to be her champion, and nothing more.

There was a soft knocking at my door.

"Come in," I said, inhaling the fragrant aroma of the night air.

I whirled to see Dawn suddenly standing at the foot of my bed. She wore a short, silky green robe that was tied at her waist. It was clear she'd thrown it on when her body was still wet from a bath or shower. The fabric clung to every curve of her body, damp in the most delicious places. Her nipples pressed enticingly, even while the cut of whatever nightclothes she wore underneath showed a generous portion of her chest.

Is this a dream—or a nightmare?

"Your cream?"

And for the first time, I saw the silver tube in her hand. *Of course, this is about preparing her champion.*

I nodded in resignation. *If all I am to her is a champion, I'm going to be the best champion I can be.* "Okay."

She gestured to the bed. "Sit down."

I did, commanding myself to feel nothing. There wasn't anything sexual about her rubbing cream all over my half-naked body, in a little robe. There was nothing sexual about her kneeling at the foot of my bed, her mouth nearly level with my cock, while I sat on the edge.

Nothing at all.

She started with my legs, rubbing gently. It seemed to me she took her time, her movements a cruel torture as she moved up. By the time she reached my thighs, my erection strained against my dark boxers. I closed my eyes, embarrassed.

The other man had offered to marry her. To give her a kind of protection I never could. She hadn't said yes, but she hadn't said no either.

And her lack of an answer? It meant that whatever I thought she was feeling for me was wrong. *Because if she felt for me what I feel for her, she would have shot him down in an instant.*

But my body didn't care about that. When she began to rub my stomach, I bit down on a groan, breathing hard. She worked the warm cream into my chest, my nipples hardening as her soft fingertips brushed over them. Then she moved to my arms.

At last, I felt her climb onto the bed behind me, goosebumps erupted over my flesh as she rubbed my back, touching every inch of me. And then, she reached forward to touch my chest once more. Her breasts rubbing against my back.

When her hands moved to my stomach, I opened my eyes. Her lips brushed my neck in a way that had every nerve in my body screaming. If she had any idea how close I was to crashing over the edge, she would've been running from the room.

Instead, her hands slid up and down my stomach and chest, at last tearing a groan from my lips. "Dawn, are we— are we done yet?"

Her hands stilled. "Do you want me to be done?"

I turned in her arms, my mouth inches from hers. God, I wanted her. Wanted to kiss her. To touch her. To know what it felt like to be inside her.

"How would Lord Jareth feel about you being in my bed right now?" The angry, jealous words came out before I could stop them.

"Aiden—"

The pity in her gaze was too much. I rose from the bed, paced for a moment, and then went back out on the balcony, waiting for her to leave.

But she didn't.

"Is he the person you were talking to when we were at the cabin that night?"

She laughed. "No. Definitely not. Jareth is just a friend. I was talking to Sammi. You remember Sammi, from high school?"

I might have remembered a quiet girl Dawn occasionally hung out with. Was that really all the phone call was about? For some reason, it didn't quiet the jealousy raging inside of me.

She came closer to me on the balcony, hesitated, then pressed into my chest, wrapping her arms around my waist.

After a moment of indecision, I held her, breathing in her sweet, fresh scent.

"I don't want to marry him. You know that right?"

I swallowed hard. "But you might."

"You don't understand."

"Of course I do. He's a rich, powerful vampire, and I'm—"

She looked up, holding my gaze, and stopping my words "—the man I love but can never be with."

I stared, lost for words. Did she just say she loved me? No, not this woman. She was too good for me. And yet, the look on her face left no room for arguments.

"Aiden, it's always been you."

My hands moved up to cup her cheeks. "Dawn."

It was all I could say. I wanted to tell her I loved her too. That I would give up anything and everything to be with her, but the words clung to the back of my throat.

She closed her eyes, her expression pained. "I'm going to agree to marry him."

My heart stopped. "No."

"Yes, I am."

Impossible. I won't allow it. "You just said you loved me."

She pressed against me even more closely. "I do."

"Then why would you marry him?"

She opened her eyes, her stunning hazel gaze pinning me into place. "Because I can't risk losing you to Draven. Jareth has agreed to fight in your place. Politically, and with both houses together, Draven can't win."

"No." I leaned closer to her, locking gazes. "I'll fight, and I'll win. And if you love me, then I will do whatever it takes to be with you."

Tears shimmered in her eyes. "I've made my decision."

But I couldn't let her go. Not when I knew she loved me. So instead, I kissed her.

For a second she held herself rigid, and then she seemed to melt in my arms. Her lips softened and spread. Her hands ran up my chest, her fingers tangling into the back of my hair.

I tilted her head, deepening our kiss. My tongue slid into her warm, inviting mouth, and she groaned against my lips. She rubbed herself against my aching cock making every nerve in my body come to life.

Tonight I would fill her completely. Tonight she would finally be mine.

And then, she broke our kiss and stumbled back. "We can't."

I reached for her, but she held her hands up to keep me away.

"Trust me enough to let me fight for you."

For one perfect second, she seemed to consider my words. And then, I heard four shots ring out. Explosions of noise that deafened the night and seemed to come from all around us.

My blood ran cold. I spun around trying to find the source of the sounds, but saw nothing, before turning to Dawn. Her eyes were wide as she stared down at herself. Four red spots slowly blossomed on her robe, and the reality of what had happened hit me.

She'd been shot.

I grabbed her, pulling her down and out of harm's way. Crouching over her, I waited for evidence of her attacker, but no one came. I inhaled deeply, trying to sense our enemy, but I was overwhelmed by the coppery scent of her blood.

She looked up at me, touching her wounds, and staring at her hands covered in blood. "Wh-what?"

A second later, the door was thrown open by Halloway. His grey hair was a bit mused, and his eyes were enraged. The old vampire looked from her to me, then zeroed in on his injured boss.

"We were on the balcony and—"

Halloway's head jerked to one side. "They're on the trail of the gunman. Keep her here with you. Feed her. And for God's sake don't let anyone disturb her tonight."

"But she's injured!"

Halloway raised one bushy brow. "Nothing that the blood of a young, healthy shifter can't fix." He turned the lock on the door and closed it behind him.

Could it really be that easy? Glancing down at Dawn, she gave a slow nod and winced. *Fuck.* I guess I still wasn't used to the supernatural world where bullet wounds like these weren't a death sentence, just another injury to heal from. I hurried across the room and closed and locked the balcony doors, staring out into the night, but all I saw were Dawn's men racing out into the woods, moving so fast that they were a blur of motion. *If the asshole who hurt her is out there, they'll find him.*

I headed back to the door to the bedroom and made certain it was locked too before looking back at the woman I loved. She lay sprawled on the ground, her eyes filled with pain. Her skin had gone several shades paler, and her hands ran over her chest and stomach lightly, as if trying to find the sources of her blood.

Ice ran through my veins. I'd never been fed on by a vampire before, but I would do anything to help Dawn, even just to take away some of her pain. But still, I was hesitant as I crossed the room back to her.

"Halloway said you just need to feed..."

She nodded, her gaze going to my throat.

Just do it. You've been through worse. "So feed." I leaned over her, but she didn't move.

"You're still healing," her voice wavered.

"I'm strong enough," I muttered.

She shook her head weakly. "No, it's not right."

Not right? What wasn't right was watching her suffer when I could help!

"Damn it! I'm more than willing!!" I tried to hide my fear with anger, sitting down beside her and pulling her closer, so that her face was close to my neck. "Drink. Feed on me. Whatever you call it."

After a second, she moaned and I felt her hot breath caress my throat.

Finally. I swallowed, imagining her teeth piercing my skin. Imagining her drinking my blood. It'd be painful, right? Like sharp needles? Like giving blood?

Hell, I had no idea.

And then, she bit down, and I bit down on a hiss of pain. But very quickly, the uncomfortable sensation faded into a warmth that spread throughout my entire body. I groaned as she rose over me and pushed me back onto the floor, as if she too was losing control.

A second later, she was straddling my hard cock. Pleasure unlike anything I'd ever felt before awakened within me, and I was lost. Lost in the feel of her slender curves pressed against my body. In the strangely sexy feeling of her teeth buried in my flesh. My hands curled around her thighs as the intoxicating warmth seemed to go on and on. Not just making me feel good, but building my arousal like I was fucking her instead of just letting her suck on me.

I felt as if I might explode, the pleasure was driving me

higher. My hips reflectively jerked upward, and my balls tightened. I tried to think of anything, anything except that Dawn was straddling me, riding me like I was her own personal mount. Except, that I couldn't escape how good it felt, and my control was slipping further and further away. *Is she going to unman me?*

She bucked above me, harder and harder, riding my manhood. Only my boxers and her underwear between us. Her breathing hard against my throat as my heart raced, and my hands ran up and down her back and shoulders, not sure what I was allowed to touch.

I was surrounded with the feel of her body, the smell of her need. *Hell, so she wants me too. Not just my blood, but my body? Fuck.* It was impossible to ignore. My vampire was turned on.

My shifter side took over. *I need her.*

But then, she drew back from me, licking the blood from her lips, and I followed her, covering her lips with my own. My blood was on her lips, so I tasted myself, her need, and something that was incredibly just Dawn all at once. It made a shudder roll through my body, so I grasped the back of her robe, trying to keep my control. Trying not to fall any harder.

Then, somehow, her robe was loose, dropping to the floor behind her.

I broke the kiss for a moment so that I could rise. Her legs wrapped around my waist as I stood. My shifter side howled at the dark green nightie she wore, the green lace transparent in the moonlight. Her nipples, small, pink, and hard peeked through, begging to be touched. I took a step toward the bed.

"Make love to me, Aiden." She gasped as she thrust against me.

I shuddered. "You're hurt."

But I still want her.

"Your blood fixed everything. I'm okay," she rubbed against my hard cock, and a string of curses exploded from my lips.

Was she still hurt? Or could she handle this?

Lifting the edges of her nightie, she pulled it off over her head, letting it flutter to the floor. My gaze went to her full bare breasts, and then to her stomach, which showed no signs of injury. Instead, her skin was stained by red, but perfect. Even her breasts were perfect. Perky, with pale pink tips, that were just begging to be touched.

"See? All better." Her voice came out husky as she took one of my hands and placed it on her breast.

I growled and carried her to the bed, my hand caressing her soft flesh. My need to take her so overwhelming that I felt like I'd taken a powerful aphrodisiac and was losing all control to it. The desire to thrust into her tight body became overwhelming. I could barely breathe as she bucked against me, trying to drive me inside her.

"Slow down, Dawn," my voice was rough. "My shifter is riding me hard to get inside you."

"Then get inside me," she whispered, reclining as I laid her back on the bed. Her arms above her head, she held my gaze as I reached down and cupped her perfect breasts.

She inhaled sharply, biting her lip, and time stood still for a moment.

Using my thumbs, I circled the nubs until they grew even harder beneath my ministrations. Then, slowly, I leaned down and took one nipple into my mouth.

She went wild, arching off the bed, grasping my head, and moaning my name. Her legs wrapped around my waist, drawing me closer. She rubbed herself eagerly against my erection, making me wild.

She reached between us and yanked my boxers down, seizing my cock and stroking its length. *Oh, shit!* A shiver went straight down my spine. *That feels so damn good.*

How many times have I imagined this? Dawn touching me. Stroking me.

"You like that?" she asked, her voice husky.

In response, a growl tore from my lips, and the primal wolf within me began to howl. I bucked in her grip as she stroked me up and down in a movement that was teasing and painful in its slowness.

If I don't distract myself, I'm going to take her hard and fast, the way my wolf wants.

But this isn't about my pleasure, it's about hers.

Ripping her panties off and tossing them to the ground, I parted her lower lips, brushing my finger along the wet folds. She gasped my name, and the sound of her slickness filled my ears, while the scent of her arousal was all around me.

Stay. In. Control.

I tried to focus on her pleasure, not on the delicate hand gripping my pulsing shaft. One of my fingers entered her channel while my thumb circled her clit. Her inner muscles squeezed me, and I shuddered, imagining those same muscles squeezing my cock. As her hands continued to pump me, I grew slick with precum. It took everything in me not to roar, tear her hand away, and slam into her wet, welcoming channel.

I was losing my mind. My control.

Her hips were rising higher and higher as she took my fingers deeper and faster. Her chest rose and fell with increasing speed. "Aiden...I'm close." She shuddered, riding my fingers harder.

Oh God, she's finally ready for me.

She whimpered when I took my hand away, but I gritted my teeth and settled on top of her, my wolf howling in triumph. *Mine.* My wolf seemed to say, and I couldn't help but agree. Dawn was ours now. Ours forever.

And then, she wrapped her legs around me again, allowing me to press closer.

The head of my cock slowly parted her lower lips, then slid into her wet channel. We both groaned together, and I closed my eyes against the barrage of pleasure that her body had stroked to life. My head fell forward. She was so tight. So wet. Her nails dug into the flesh of my shoulder, urging me on.

I sank, inch by inch, deeper and deeper into her, until I came to my hilt. There, I paused, overwhelmed by my senses, trying to keep some semblance of control. My muscles strained with the effort of holding back. Of giving her tight body time to grow accustomed to my girth. But, still, I waited. Remembering how much she had been through, and never wanting to cause her any pain.

My job was to take her pain away, not cause it.

When her grip on my shoulders lessened, I looked at her, holding her gaze as I slowly pulled back out. Her mouth dropped open in an unspoken *O*, and her nails dug into my flesh once more. I shivered, loving the sensation of my shaft being held so tightly by her body. Loving the raw desire and wonder in her gaze.

I'm making her feel this way. Me...this is unbelievable.

When only my tip remained inside her, I hesitated a moment, then plunged back in. We groaned together, and then, my control snapped. I pounded into her wet, welcoming body. The sounds of her desire filling my ears. Her moans growing louder and louder. Her legs shook, her body shuddering beneath me with each of my thrusts.

She's close. So close. As was I.

She pressed her lips against my neck and then sank her teeth into me. My shock was immediately replaced with pure pleasure. Wrapping one hand behind her head, I drew her closer. Feeling nothing but my cock pressed deep into her body. Feeling nothing but the heat spiraling from her bite.

And then, I came back to myself. Her channel was so wet, so ready. Her legs holding me so deeply that I could go no further.

Gritting my teeth, I began to thrust again. Harder and harder.

We immediately found a rhythm. Her teeth still sunk into my flesh. Her legs wrapped around me as she pulled me closer, forcing me deeper.

My hands clenched the bedsheets, pounding into her as I felt myself moving closer to the edge. My pleasure building until at last she screamed and shuddered around me. I forgot to breathe as I felt her coming. My name escaped her lips again, and something shattered inside of me.

I exploded, feeling her orgasm continue as I came too, my hot seed filling her body. Claiming her as my own. It felt like the very earth had opened up and swallowed us whole, pulling us into a place where only she and I and this moment existed.

It was impossible to stop. I just continued sliding in and out of her for several minutes as we shuddered together. At last, I collapsed on top of her. *My Dawn is incredible.*

"That was...so good," she whispered.

I looked down at her. Her eyes had closed, her face relaxed in sleep.

Unable to help myself, I kissed her soft lips. *From this day forward you are mine. Mine to love. And mine to protect.*

Rolling to her side, I pulled her close to me, covered our bodies with a blanket, and drifted into the most peaceful sleep of my life.

23

DAWN

I OPENED MY EYES, feeling confused and out of place. I was in a familiarly soft bed, but something felt different. And then I realized there was a warm body beneath my hand. Looking up, I stared into Aiden's sleeping face. Memories of the night came back to me. Sex with Aiden had been so good it was almost unreal. I should logically regret our night together, but somehow, I couldn't bring myself to. In any other situation, I would have blamed it on the pleasure a bite could bring, but we both knew it was more than that.

I need to find a way to keep him, and *to keep him out of danger. Is such a thing even possible?*

Slipping out of bed, I put on my clothes and left his room. Trying to distract myself, I showered, did my hair and makeup, and put on my most comfortable clothes. The well-made white jeans hugged my body in all the right places. And my top? Well, it was pure art. Long in the front and back, it nearly reached my knees. But on the sides? It slit up high, revealing peeks of my flesh between the stripes of black fabric. The high neckline in front made the sexy dip in the back even more fun.

Putting on my short black-and-white leather boots, I stepped out into the hall and met a world of chaos. *That's right. I was shot.*

How could sex with Aiden make me forget that? My inner muscles tightened in memory. *Oh. That's how.*

Halloway instantly raced up to me and made his report. By the time they caught up to the shifter who had shot me, his throat had been torn open by some kind of wild animal. Perhaps even another shifter, which was just bizarre. Vampires and shifters had always had a tense history, but it wasn't often one shifter killed another shifter, at least not around here.

The notion didn't sit well with my head of security, but I did my best to reassure him.

"Dawn, this was a warning. If they'd meant to kill you, they would have used something other than a gun. This was to show you that you're not even safe in your own home." He covered his face with his hands, more upset than I'd ever seen him. "You should replace me."

Replace him? Yeah right. "Halloway, there *is* no one better than you. It's going to be fine. I'm a tough girl to kill."

I could see Halloway disagreed, but he held his tongue.

Next came the chief of police, a shifter with a constant scowl on his face. Apparently, twelve people had gone missing since my trip to Ghost Town, and the police force suspected vampires were to blame. Again, I tried to reassure him. But his warning to take care of the problem was less of a suggestion and more a warning.

Which *I* didn't appreciate.

Our relationship with the human police in Mist had

been solid since my brother took over. They realized that, if the government learned of the vampires' presence in Mist, we would be removed. And if we left, this place would fall apart. Most humans, unless given positions by supernaturals, were poor and suffering. Our "donations" kept the humans of this town thriving.

It was a symbiotic relationship. If we disappeared, the humans would suffer. If we were forced out of here, we would suffer. Everyone knew this, and yet, twelve missing humans in a world where human numbers were dwindling? It meant trouble.

By the time I was finished dealing with the responsibilities of my household, it was nearly nightfall once more. I sipped a glass of warm blood and made my way up to Aiden's room, hoping he'd returned from the security detail Halloway had insisted he shadow.

Time for us to discuss last night.

Turning the handle on his door, I opened it a crack and knocked softly.

A soft beeping caught my ear.

"Come in," he said, his voice filled with excitement.

I entered, frowning, and closing the door behind me.

He was standing staring down at something in his hand.

As I got closer I recognized the communications device. "What is it doing?"

Looking up at me, his expression was one of shock. "It's telling me that a ship is passing between realms."

I thought we had three or four more days.

I slid closer to him, staring down at a screen with a dot blinking in and out over our world. "Are they getting your message?"

"No," he said, frowning, "but this tiny monitor indicated a place I can get a clearer signal."

"Where?"

"It looks to be about thirty minutes from here."

Looking down at the screen, I instantly recognized the spot. *Boulder Creek*. "That's a wooded area. We'll gather a team and—"

He looked up for the first time, his gaze sweeping over me in a way that made me blush. "Sorry, but you're staying here. Where it's safe."

I huffed. "You do realize I was shot here last night. Four times. In the chest."

"Doesn't matter," he said stubbornly. "Halloway said this is the safest place for you to be and that you need every last vampire on guard to keep you protected. I'm going now, and I'm going alone."

"Like hell you are!"

He grabbed my arm and pulled me against him, his hard mouth crushing mine in a kiss that sent my head spinning. Unable to help myself, I relaxed against him. Aiden was many things, one of which was an amazing kisser. I wonder what else that amazing mouth of his could do...I swore I would find out.

Then, he pulled back, a low growl emanating from his chest. "You're staying here."

I shook myself, trying to clear my head. Aiden had been through a lot in his life, the last thing he needed was to put himself in more dangerous positions than he had to.

"I'm sorry, but no. I'm not," I replied calmly.

He was breathing hard, his mouth brushing my cheeks and moving on to my neck. I shifted closer to him, desire uncurling in my belly as I felt his obvious arousal.

"If I go alone, I can be back before anyone notices. If I take you with me, I'm sure your enemies will follow."

Damn it. He's right about that. But the idea of letting him go alone made me feel uneasy.

I took a deep breath, deciding on a compromise. "All right. But you're taking Edger and Soren with you." He lifted a brow like he thought I was crazy. "The two young vampires might look inexperienced, but they can fight like hell if they need to."

After a long moment, he sighed. "Okay, but I have to leave now." He kissed me one last time, then headed down the stairs.

I followed, still unsure that I should let him go.

After giving a few commands to my staff, Edger and Soren joined us, looking excited to be included. They were jumping around, grinning, so tired of the usual calm of Darkmore Manor. Aiden moved closer to me, as if he might kiss me again, but then glanced at my staff and pulled away. Regret filled my stomach as our eyes locked, silently wanting him to know just how much I cared for him. He nodded, as if he understood, then I turned away. He and the two blond vampires slipped out into the night while I stood in the doorway of my home, staring after them long after they were gone.

Be safe, I prayed.

A half-hour later, as I was sorting through paperwork in my office, my private line rang. I picked it up absentmindedly, too distracted by Aiden's absence to consider much else.

"Do you know where your mutt is?" Draven's voice came over the line, cold and cruel.

Fuck. I had been worried about the warlocks, but never about the other vampires. Our society had rules, rules that most of us followed. But, of course, Draven thought he was above the rules.

"Listen, you bastard, if you—"

"He was an idiot to double-cross those warlocks. They're dangerous, and that's coming from me. Too bad my Tracker led them right to him."

"Not possible."

"Oh, but unfortunately for us all, it is. And I have a feeling if you don't find your mutt soon, he'll be warlock chow."

My heart in my throat, I listened as the line went dead.

"Halloway!" I screamed. Rising from my seat, I rushed toward the door.

It might be a trap. That was the most logical answer, rather than the warlocks being bold enough to attack Aiden on my own lands, now that I knew about them. But I didn't care. Trap or not, I would get Aiden back safely.

No matter the cost.

24

AIDEN

I STOOD at the top of the large white rock surrounded by a thick forest, the two vampires a short distance away. Above me, thunder shook the night air. That was one thing I'd forgotten about Mist, how volatile the weather could be. The sound of the rushing river behind us filled the silence the thunder had left behind. I needed to hurry, not just because I worried the warlocks would know the ship was passing close to us soon, but also because I wasn't sure how the device would hold up in the rain, and the sky definitely promised a terrible storm.

Holding the communication device as high as I could, I was rewarded when it made a soft chime. *Success! It has found a signal!*

I clicked a button on the device and my prerecorded message began. "To whoever hears this message: Dangerous warlock shifters have escaped from prison and landed in my realm. They are known criminals in whatever world they came from and were hunted by beings called the Magic Police. They are attempting to create warlock-human hybrids. If they are not removed from this world, the damage they could inflict would be costly. Please come and collect them."

Then, the message began again.

The two young vampires who had accompanied me leaned against the boulder looking bored. I had a feeling when we set out for this mission they'd wanted fighting and danger. Ages were sometimes hard to tell with supernaturals, but they looked to be roughly in their early twenties, with a thirst for adventure, and not a lot of patience.

"How much longer?" Edger, the grumpy one, asked, as if reading my thoughts.

I grinned, already feeling as if a weight had been lifted off of my shoulders. "Just until I'm sure someone got it."

Then, my grin faded, and I inhaled deeply. Just a little, below the scents of the river and the forest, was a familiar, unwelcome scent. It was muted, but definitely there. The odd smell of the warlock shifters.

I sniffed again, confirming what I already knew. "Guys, we've got trouble."

They instantly snapped to attention, their hands curling into fists. Their gazes went to the woods behind us, searching the shadows as if their keen eyes could pick out trouble as quickly as a wolf's sense of smell.

"What is it?" Soren asked, his eyes searching the woods.

"Warlock shifters. I can smell them."

Edger's fists dropped and he twisted around to glare up at me. "Really funny. Have you ever heard of the boy who cried wolf, because—"

One of the shifters leaped out of the darkness, latching onto Edgar's throat and pulling him to the ground. The sounds of his gurgling filled the darkness, and the stench of blood hit my nostrils.

Fuck.

The other vampire jumped onto the back of the wolf, twisting his head until it snapped. The warlock slumped to the ground, dead. Then, Soren knelt down beside his friend, looking panicked.

Placing his hands over his friend's throat, the vampire stared up at me, his eyes wide. "We need to get him help! Now!" He hesitated, his voice cracking as he continued. "Should I try to feed him now or wait to get him somewhere safer?"

I doubt we'll make it to safety at all, but if the shifters surround us here, we're dead.

"Let me think." I glanced down at the communications device. Scrawled in an unusual font across the front it said *Communication Received.*

"Hopefully I reached the right person," I muttered angrily.

Knowing that it was too dangerous to leave the item when the warlock shifters were closing in on us, I snapped the device in my hand, hoping I hadn't just doomed our realm. Then, cracked the communicator in pieces a few more times for good measure. *Now, they have no chance of ever reaching their boss. And as long as I reached the Magic Police, they should be picked up soon, and our realm will be free of them at last.*

Dropping the pieces, I reached for my clothes, undressing in a rush.

"What are you doing?"

I looked at the young vampire. *So much life ahead of him.* "I'm going to shift and lead them away from you. And you,

you're going to try your best to keep yourself and your friend alive."

The vampire nodded, unspoken gratitude in his eyes.

I usually hated to shift—it represented everything those warlock criminals had done to me. But at that moment, I embraced it. My spine cracked, and I felt the horrific pain that accompanied the changing of my body structure. My thoughts went dark for a long moment, and then, the world around me looked different. Muted in grays.

In my wolf form, I could smell the warlocks even better, and they were too damn close for my liking. Picking the path that led away from town, I started running, careful to brush every damn tree and bush along the way. I needed to lead them straight to me, to even give the young vampires a chance to get away.

And then, then I needed to run like hell to a safe place.

25

AIDEN

ONLY A FEW MINUTES had passed when I sensed them closing in on me, gaining on me as they spread out on all sides. I ran harder, pushing myself even as my wolf protested. Being cautious, I slowly switched my angle, heading for Mist. With all the creatures that lived there, I was sure to find help somewhere.

When I saw the first lights of the city up ahead, I had one moment to feel like I might just make it, before a heavy body crashed into me. I rolled, taking the wolf with me. It latched onto my back, sinking sharp teeth into my shoulder.

I shook the wolf free, then turned to face him. The wolf leaped again, and at the last minute I twisted, latching onto the wolf's throat with my sharp fangs.

With a howl of pain, my enemy slumped onto the ground.

I bit harder, crushing his windpipe, not stopping until

the beast took its final breath. Then I rose. Five steps later, two warlock shifters crowded in front of me.

I snarled, showing my teeth. Together, they rushed me. Teeth and claws slashed at me, but I was bigger, stronger, and faster. I clawed and bit as they came at me over and over again. But no matter how much they tried to defeat me, I wouldn't allow it. I'd sent the message. Now, I needed to be Dawn's champion. And once she was safe, we could be together. I just had to deal with these assholes first.

A wolf leaped at me again, and I ducked, then bit down hard on his paw. He made a terrible sound of pain, and I released him, jumping back and watching. Waiting for the next attack. Instead, he made a low whining noise and limped away, his paw badly mangled, while the other wolf lay in the darkness of the forest floor, struggling for breath.

I knew there were more of them in the woods, so I barely gave them another glance before continuing toward town. *I have to get back to Dawn.*

When I stepped out into a clearing, I made it halfway through before sensing movement behind me. I spun, but then caught movement on both my sides. My heart raced as I slowly realized what had happened.

They had surrounded me. *This cannot happen. I'm her champion.*

Aghader approached me but paused a distance away. He shifted and stood, a naked man with long dark hair and a white eye that glowed. "Tell me where to find the device, and we'll let you live."

I'll have a better chance in my human form.

I shifted back, swallowing my scream of pain as I rose unsteadily to my feet. "By the stream."

Aghader's good eye narrowed. "All we found were

broken pieces of what looked like a communications device."

Shit.

"But we assumed that no creature would be so stupid as to destroy his only hope of survival."

I put a hand over a wound on my arm and realized it was dripping too quickly. I blinked when my head began to feel light. Fighting the shifters, I'd been so focused on escaping and getting back to Dawn I'd barely noticed the injuries I'd attained. But standing here, they were impossible to ignore. I needed to keep going, before it was too late.

"Say something!" the warlock demanded.

I looked around myself at the pack of angry warlock shifters. *There are too many of them. I'm too badly wounded. Damn it. I'm going to die this time.*

Swallowing, I met the eyes of the man I hated. "You destroyed my life. It was only fitting that I destroyed yours."

Raw hatred twisted the warlock's face. "Kill him! Tear him to—"

A bright golden light suddenly surrounded Aghader. His mouth pulled into a scream, and then, he was gone.

I looked up to see light reflect off the surface of a large white ship, its billowing sails giving it the look of a ghost ship. *They're here!*

A second later, the blue light slid over another warlock, and he too disappeared. Which is when chaos was unleashed. The wolves scattered, running every which way, and the ship seemed to follow the groups without urgency. My satisfaction faded as I watched another wolf get taken.

What's to keep them from taking me, too?

Turning, I limped toward the town. *I survived, and Dawn is safe. That's all that matters.*

And then, I heard a scream.

26

*D*AWN

M*Y* CAR SKIDDED to the stop in the middle of the town as the clouds overhead flashed with lightning. "What happened?" I called from the back seat. "Why did we stop?"

I frowned, glancing out my window, searching for my security detail in the shadows. One of my vampires stepped out into the light, the mist moving through the streets seemed to gather more thickly around him. I felt a wave of relief, and then, a blade sliced his throat from behind.

His body fell to the ground.

"Halloway! Pierce!" I screamed, rolling down the screen between me and my security.

In the front seat, both men were dead, their throats slit, and their doors thrown open.

Yet all was quiet.

How did this happen in an instant? Without me hearing or seeing anything?

It wasn't the work of just one vampire.

Clenching my hands into fists, I opened my door and stepped out. From every corner and every shadow, Draven's men seemed to melt into existence. My own men were nowhere to be found. *Please don't be dead. Just be imprisoned somewhere.* But I had a feeling if Draven was involved, they hadn't shown my men any mercy.

The night was deadly silent, as if every bird, bug, and beast knew not to make a sound. That the vampires were on the loose.

This can't be happening.

"You're making a mistake," I shouted. "Whatever he promised you, it isn't enough. The people in Mist *are* your people now. You can't just flip a switch and start seeing them as food again."

Not a single vampire reacted to my words. They simply stared. Overhead, lightning split the night sky, followed by an ominous rumble of thunder. *So this will end just how it began.*

I spun slowly taking in the sheer number of vampires who surrounded me. *There must be fifty of them. At least.* A chill raced down my spine. *My death won't be a quick one.*

"There's still time." I tried to keep the desperation out of my voice. "Think about what my family has done for you. Is this really how you think this should end?"

No one answered, but I could feel the tension in the air. *What are they waiting for?*

Then, as if in answer, a slow clapping split the silence.

My eyes jerked toward the sound.

Draven stepped into the street in front of my car. A dozen vampires formed a tight line behind him. Even some that I had once called allies. *Is this what we've been reduced to? Turning on one another...for what? To return to the days where vampires ruled with terror.*

I glanced back and saw that another line of vampires was closing in behind my car. And on each side of me.

"Are you serious? All of you?" My voice rose with incredulity. "My brother cared for you, kept the peace. Even I've helped most of you over the years." My eyes met Jana's. "I looked up to you as a sister when we were in school. Do you really believe we—those of us who care for all creatures, magical or human—deserve to die?"

Jana looked away, unable to meet my gaze. But I didn't back away.

I planted my feet firmly on the ground, prepared to fight. *The odds don't look good,* I had to admit.

Draven's clapping stopped as he froze, not twenty feet in front of me. "Congratulations on making it here in one piece, but that my dear, was too easy. Luring you out of your little fortress, killing every single one of the people who were mistakenly protecting you...and all for the sake of one pathetic freak."

I felt sick for a moment. *All those people. They didn't deserve to die.* My anger rose. "Our challenge was set for tomorrow. My champion would have met you fairly on the battlefield."

He laughed and, with a small jump, landed on the hood of my car. "Well, with your challenger dead, I thought why bother waiting?"

I narrowed my eyes. "Aiden isn't dead. You're lying." I held my hand up and pretended to examine my nails. "You must be pretty afraid to disobey the ancient rules of a challenge. To ambush and kill my people," I said, glancing at him out of the corner of my eye, and letting my voice dripped with sarcasm. "Was it performance anxiety? Afraid you couldn't do it in a fair fight?"

My gaze went to the vampires surrounding me, seeking a

friendly face, and finding none. *You thought you could control them, Liam, make them civilized. Obviously, there was a side to them you didn't know.* We *didn't know.*

Draven's expression twisted with fury. "We'll see who's scared now, won't we? One last chance, Dawn. Marry me. A vampire as beautiful as you needn't die for a pathetic notion of love. Be my bride and we will rule the houses through our might and power!"

How wrong you are, Draven. Might and power bring fear, not loyalty. Instead of saying my thoughts aloud though, I simply smiled. "How it must bother you—to know I'd rather die than be your wife." My teeth lengthened, my legs tensing as I prepared to fight.

A commotion came from behind the line of vampires, and I heard someone cry out, "It's the shifter!"

I caught a glimpse of Aiden behind them. Limping. Bleeding. *He's alive!* My heart rose.

The instant Aiden spotted me, then slid to my attackers, a look of fury came over his face, and he shifted into a wolf in seconds. Only, his wolf kept growing. He doubled in size, his fur turning a bright white only obscured by the blood from his many wounds. Instead of a shifter, he looked like something out of a fantasy world. Certainly not a creature that belonged here.

A warlock hybrid. Is that what their powers created in a human?

"What the fuck?" Someone shouted.

"What is that?"

A murmur went up, and I heard Aiden growl low in the back of his throat.

"It's just a shifter you idiots!" Draven screamed. "Kill him. I'll deal with her myself."

The vampires, obviously so fueled with violence and

bloodlust that they were beyond reason, headed straight for Aiden. I knew the moment Aiden realized it, but he could do nothing to stop the dozens of vampires who swarmed him. Except to fight with every last drop of strength he possessed.

They're going to kill him in minutes.

I turned my gaze to Draven.

He smiled. "Killing him will be as easy as killing your weak brother."

Ice slid down my spine. "Y-you didn't. He was murdered by dark magic. Some evil creature, not of this world."

"Perhaps, like warlocks who can shift into any form? A being that one minute looks like an innocent creature in need, and when they were alone, tore him to pieces?"

My hand clutched at my chest. I couldn't breathe.

Of course Draven was behind it. I'd been so busy trying to survive that I hadn't considered how my brother and this traitor could be connected. *I'm a fool.*

"I'm going to kill you," I promised.

The snarls of the vampires surrounding Aiden came to me, and I turned to look in their direction. He was fighting like a rabid animal, but he couldn't keep them at bay much longer. *I have to reach him, before it's too late.*

Instinct made me duck just as a ball of fire flew through the air and landed an inch away from me. Flames exploded on the hood of my car and I realized Draven had jumped off. I scanned the area, finding him behind me.

Breathing hard, I crouched, staring at the man who had turned my world upside down. Who killed my brother, Halloway, and the others. Who had almost caused the downfall of the Darkmore legacy.

My throat closed. *Who had ordered his people to kill Aiden. He deserved to die.*

Three fireballs barreled toward me, but I avoided each one with ease, slowly making my way closer to him. In his arrogance, he only laughed, unaware that I was doing more than surviving. I was going to kill him.

If I don't kill him, he's going to do this to countless others. Drawing the vampires into bloodlust, feeding and killing at his leisure.

As my anger grew, something within me swelled. Heating. Changing. I felt it radiating through my blood, through my bones, through my heart. And for the first time, I was glad to feel that dangerous energy inside of me.

When I was a foot from Draven, my hand began to glow with a bold red color. I couldn't see it, but I sure as hell felt it, and knew exactly what it would look like. Still, I hid it behind me until I was inches from him.

Then moving with deadly intent, I reached out and grabbed him.

He noticed it too late, his eyes widening as death closed in on him. "But you..."

I felt the life flee his body as I touched him, and then he slumped to the ground. *That's right. The Lady of Death has returned.*

Certain he was dead, I whirled and rushed toward the vampires who snarled and growled, as they fed on Aiden, who was now in his human form. Vulnerable. I couldn't even imagine how badly he'd been injured to no longer be a wolf.

It scared me.

Without hesitation, I reached out, carving a path of death through them. "Aiden," I cried feverishly, "hold on!" I touched one after another of my enemies, dropping them where they stood. *But no matter how fast I kill them, I can't get through them fast enough.*

Once they began to notice, my presence cut through their bloodlust, sending the living vampires fleeing, taking off into the shadows.

Until I at last reached Aiden.

He was still, covered in blood. Unmoving.

Collapsing to my knees, my throat tight with unshed tears, I reached for his blood-soaked neck. There was no pulse.

"No!" I screamed into the night. *It's not possible.* I began to sob, clutching his lifeless body to my chest. Staring down at the man I loved. The man I had always loved.

High above me, a shadow blocked out the moonlight. Staring up through eyes filled with tears, I saw the white ship. It was the same shape as the one we'd found in the desert. A white light fell over me and Aiden, blinding me.

For one horrible instant, I wondered what else they would do, but the light disappeared and the ship shot away.

They wanted to take him too, I thought numbly. *But I guess they have no use for a body.*

I sobbed harder, pressing my face into Aiden's hair. *I don't want to be the touch of death! All I want is to save him!*

And even though I hadn't touched him, I had killed him just as surely as I killed my parents. I had pulled him into my world. I was responsible for his death.

Death was my only companion. It always had been. *Liam was the light twin—I am the dark. The vampire cursed.*

Crying harder, I imagined a world without him in it. A dark world full of emptiness. "I need you," I sobbed brokenly. "I don't want to do this without you."

I looked into his sightless eyes, and an anger I had never felt came from deep within my core. *I don't want to be the dark twin anymore!*

I clenched my fists in rage. *I want to bring life!*

"You're going to live, damn it!" I cried, pressing my hands against his chest. With all of my heart, I willed him to live. No matter the cost. No matter the consequence. I willed for him to come back to me.

A tingle spread through my body, a coldness that froze my blood. My breath puffed out, a cloud of white. The hands that touched his chest began to glow. Not red, but gold.

And then the impossible happened.

His wounds began to heal. His skin stitched up before my eyes, the blood pooling and running back into his body. The dirt washing clean from his flesh. His whole chest shuddered, then expanded with a great intake of air. The breath that exploded from his lips was noisy. And the most wonderful sound in the world.

Rain began to tumble down, as if a curtain had fallen around us. We were drenched in an instant, but I didn't care. My gaze was trained on him as his dark-lashed eyes opened, and then came to focus on me.

"Wh-what happened?" His voice was groggy.

I was crying too hard to speak. Instead, I watched as the glowing in my hands faded. Then, wrapping my arms around him, I held him so tight, willing him to never leave me again.

"You brought me back," he whispered.

I pulled back from him a little and shook my head. "But I can't. My touch only brings death."

He reached up and stroked my face. "Not this time.

How had this happened? I was supposed to bring death, not life.

The rain in front of us suddenly began to swirl together until it took a form. *The goddess of the rain.* She was young, with skin the iridescent white-blue of rain, and a dress that shone like the dew on a flower's petal.

The goddess knelt down, brushing a wet hand against my cheek. "The earth has sensed in you more than death since the very beginning."

So I saved him? My touch actually saved someone.

My eyes filled with tears once more. "Did all of you know? Did you always know?"

She smiled, her face kind. "Always. You, our daughter, who has had a lifetime of pain. Now, you will have a lifetime of happiness. It won't be easy, nothing worth having ever is, but it will be happy."

I brushed the tears that streamed down my face away, holding Aiden's hand tightly in my own. "Thank you."

The goddess straightened. "It was your own strength that did this, not mine." She blew Dawn a soft kiss, then exploded into a rush of rain that hit the pavement without a sound.

I looked down at the man in my arms, whose gaze held mine. "I love you."

The confusion in his face fled. "I love you too."

I stroked his hair, glorying in the sight of him. In the knowledge that everything keeping us apart was gone. And that we could have a future together, if he wanted.

"How would you feel about being the Lord of Darkmore?"

The corners of his mouth lifted into a brilliant smile. "You can call this poor hybrid anything you want, as long as I'm yours." But then, his smile faltered. "There was a ship, hunting the warlocks, I think it might—"

"It came, but left when it found you dead."

The worry instantly left his face. "I wondered if it might

see a warlock hybrid as one of them. I guess I was lucky they didn't get their hands on me."

I grinned. "So, the warlocks are gone. Humanity is safe. And Draven's been defeated. I think this might just be our happily ever after."

He stroked my cheek. "And we have each other."

"That's the best part of all."

We kissed, there in the rain, knowing that nothing could ever keep us apart again.

27

SAMMI

MY PHONE RANG, and I rolled over in bed with a groan. *Hadn't dealing with the orc been enough? But no, a Human Defender's job is never truly done.* I smacked at the phone a couple of times before I pulled it to me and stared at the name, so exhausted and sore it hurt to breathe.

Sigh. I answered the phone. "Hey, Dawn, how are you doing?"

My friend's voice came over the line. "Actually, really well. Sorry to call you so late."

"Nah, you're good. What's up?"

I had a feeling I knew why she was calling. To make sure I wasn't investigating her brother's death too much. But luckily for her, I knew better than to stick my nose in Mist's business. Other people might not know how dangerous that was, but I'd grown up there, I knew asking too many questions would get me killed, so I just didn't.

She sounded excited. "I just wanted to tell you we found my brother's killer and dealt with him."

I sat up. "Dealt with him?"

"I just didn't want you to worry about it," she rushed out.

Glancing around, I lowered my voice. "Dawn, just be careful. They're cracking down more and more on vampires. If they find out you're in Mist, you're screwed."

"You know what I am?" I could almost hear her heart racing even over the line.

Since we were young this secret, and others, had hung between us. This was the first time I felt like it was smarter just to say it than to leave it unsaid between us. If she was reckless, my friend could get in trouble right now. Because even though I didn't get involved with Mist, even I'd heard the whispers about missing humans recently.

"Yeah, I know what you are, and the government will probably focus on our town for a little while, so be extra careful. I'd hate to see Mist destroyed."

"But you're not going to tell anyone?"

I guessed it was time. "The thing is, I'm not exactly human myself, so I don't really have a leg to stand on."

"No way."

"Way," I said with a grin. "I'm *technically* a succubus."

"A succubus?" she sounded shocked. "But you hid it so well!"

"You did a pretty damn good job yourself." In fact, if I had actually been human, I never would've suspected the truth. But being supernatural myself, I'd always known Dawn and her family were vampires.

The thing is, they kept more humans alive in my home-town than the government had managed to do anywhere else. So even though I was required by law to tell the authorities about the vampires, I wouldn't. Because I didn't become a Human Defender for the red tape. I became one to help people.

Despite what humans sometimes think.

"You keep things safe there for the humans," I told her, "no one ever needs to know the truth."

Dawn laughed, sounding relieved. "Deal."

I hesitated, my bed calling to me. "Was there something else?"

I know there is...

"You remember how I found Aiden?" There was a smile in her voice.

"The hottie you not so secretly had a crush on? Yeah."

She sounded embarrassed. "Well, we're...we're together now."

I smiled, even though my heart ached. "That's really wonderful."

"I never thought," she started, then stopped for a moment before continuing. "I never thought I would find anyone. I mean, there are some things to work out, but it feels like anything is possible."

"I'm so glad for you," I said, and I meant it. Dawn deserved to be happy.

"How are you doing?" she asked, and some of the joy left her voice.

"Work is good."

What else could I say? That secretly I was dying of loneliness? That being a Human Defender in one of the hardest cities in the country was my whole life? It was pathetic.

"What about *that* guy?"

Luke. A man I had fallen so hard and so fast for at the Human Defender's academy that I'd really thought a succubus might find love.

Idiot.

I was wrong. Of course, I was wrong. And now that guy was gone. Ancient history. And I was alone, pretending at night that I didn't miss a man who had made it very clear that he hated me.

"Sammi?"

I stiffened, realizing it'd been a while since I last answered. "I still haven't heard from him. But I'm sure if I do, it'll only be to remind me how much he hates me."

"Oh, I am so sorry."

"It's okay," I forced myself to sound happy. "I'm just glad you found your guy and the answer to some of your questions. You deserve all the best things in the world."

"You too." And a little giggle escaped her lips.

"Is he there with you?" I asked, smirking.

"Yeah," she said, "and I guess he wants my attention."

I laughed. "Okay, go have fun."

We said goodbye, and the line went dead. I dropped my phone onto my stomach and stared up at the ceiling. I wasn't lonely. Not *that* lonely. Work was good. I had friends. I didn't really need more than that.

Liar.

My phone beeped, and I sighed as I pulled up my new text message. Work was calling.

No surprise there...

Time to kick some ass.

ALSO BY LACEY CARTER ANDERSEN

Guild of Assassins

Mercy's Revenge

Mercy's Fall

Monsters and Gargoyles

Medusa's Destiny *audiobook*

Keto's Tale

Celaeno's Fate

Cerberus Unleashed

Lamia's Blood

Shade's Secret

Hecate's Spell

Empusa's Hunger

Shorts: Their Own Sanctuary

Shorts: Their Miracle Pregnancy

Dark Supernaturals

Wraith Captive

Marked Immortals

Chosen Warriors

Wicked Reform School/House of Berserkers

Untamed: Wicked Reform School

Unknown: House of Berserkers

Unstable: House of Berserkers

Royal Fae Academy

Revere (A Short Prequel)

Ravage

Ruin

Reign

Box Set: Dark Fae Queen

Immortal Hunters MC

Van Helsing Rising

Van Helsing Damned

Magical Midlife in Mystic Hollow

Karma's Spell

Karma's Shift

Infernal Queen

Raising Hell

Fresh Hell

Straight to Hell

Her Demon Lovers

Secret Monsters

Unchained Magic

Dark Powers

Box Set: Mate to the Demon Kings

An Angel and Her Demons

Supernatural Lies

Immortal Truths

Lover's Wrath

Box Set: Fallen Angel Reclaimed

Legacy of Blood and Magic

Dragon Shadows

Dragon Memories

Legends Unleashed

Don't Say My Name

Don't Cross My Path

Don't Touch My Men

The Firehouse Feline

Feline the Heat

Feline the Flames

Feline the Burn

Feline the Pressure

God Fire Reform School

Magic for Dummies

Myths for Half-Wits

Mayhem for Suckers

Box Set: God Fire Academy

The Icelius Reverse Harem

Her Alien Abductors

Her Alien Barbarians

Her Alien Mates

ABOUT THE AUTHOR

Lacey Carter Andersen is a USA Today bestselling author who loves reading, writing, and drinking excessive amounts of coffee. She spends her days taking care of her husband, three kids, and three cats. But at night, everything changes! Her imagination runs wild with strong-willed characters, unique worlds, and exciting plots that she enthusiastically puts into stories.

Lacey has dozens of tales: science fiction romances, paranormal romances, short romances, reverse harem romances, and more. So, please feel free to dive into any of her worlds; she loves to have the company!

And you're welcome to reach out to her; she really enjoys hearing from her readers.

You can find her at:

Email: laceycarterandersen@gmail.com

Mailing List:

https://www.subscribepage.com/laceycarterandersen

Website: https://laceycarterandersen.net/

Facebook Page: https://www.facebook.com/authorlaceycarterandersen

ALSO BY MELANIE GREY

Court of Magic: Vampires
Chosen by Blood

ABOUT THE AUTHOR

Melanie Grey is a writer of paranormal romance who enjoys strong heroines and the men who love them. Her books are filled with adventure, romance, and lots of spice.

Printed in Great Britain
by Amazon